CW00666075

T
EIGHTH
BLACK BOOK
OF
HORROR

Selected by Charles Black

Mortbury Press

Published by Mortbury Press

First Edition
2011

ISBN 978-0-9556061-7-5

Mortbury Press
Shiloh
Nantglas
Llandrindod Wells
Powys
LD1 6PD

mortburypress@yahoo.com
http://mortburypress.webs.com/
http://twitter.com/mortburypress

Contents

Dedicated to Richard Davis

*****

Acknowledgements

Quieta Non Movere © by Reggie Oliver 2011
The Last Coach Trip © by David A. Riley 2011
Home by the Sea © by Stephen Bacon 2011
Boys Will be Boys © by David Williamson 2011
Behind the Screen © by Gary Fry 2011
The Other Tenant © by Mark Samuels 2011
Tok © by Paul Finch 2011
Little Pig © by Anna Taborska 2011
Casualties of the System © by Tina & Tony Rath 2011
How the Other Half Die © by John Llewellyn Probert 2011
Music in the Bone © by Marion Pitman 2011
The Coal-Man © by Thana Niveau 2011
Mea Culpa © by Kate Farrell 2011

Cover artwork © by Paul Mudie 2011

*****

Also in this series:
Seven more volumes of unadulterated *HORROR!*

QUIETA NON MOVERE

Reggie Oliver

One of my first clerical positions was that of a curate to a parish just outside the cathedral city of Morchester. Being of a naturally studious inclination, I devoted my spare time to researching the history of the district and, in particular, the cathedral. I even proposed to write a short monograph on some of the more curious funerary monuments to be found in that building. One in particular attracted my attention because of its strange inscription and carving. My enquiries about this particular monument elicited a story of some very shocking events connected with that tomb which happened some ten years previous to my arrival in Morchester. Despite the passing of a decade, the events were still very clear in the minds of those who witnessed them and who were willing to speak to me. Their accounts are the foundations of the story I am about to tell.

Let me therefore remove you a while to the ancient city of Morchester in the County of Morsetshire in the year 1863. Though the railway had arrived some fifteen years previously, it could be said that in all other respects time had stood still in the city for many decades. It had been and remained a prosperous market town; it boasted a fine cathedral, mostly in the Early English and Decorated styles. Rooks cawed among its towers and in the immemorial elms that punctuated the sward of its fine old close.

One cloudless afternoon in the July of that year the great bell of the Cathedral began to sound its bass note, summoning the city to the funeral of one of its servants. The Dean was dead. That ancient knell, that call to remembrance, and reminder of mortality, would no doubt have seemed to Morchester's inhabitants no more than a slight eddy in the changeless flow of life and death which washed about its walls. Who could have foreseen that it tolled the commencement of a series of

5

horribly inexplicable events?

In all conscience, the passing of The Very Rev. William Ainsley, Dean of Morchester was greeted with little sadness, and was the occasion, in some quarters, of no small relief. Dean Ainsley had for many years been infirm and fulfilled his decanal duties with a listlessness only just short of rank incompetence. When, on the day of his funeral, the Very Rev. Stephen Coombe acceded to the position and sat in his stall in the choir, there was much talk of new brooms sweeping clean. Even those who did not find such a metaphor entirely reassuring were compelled to admit that anything was preferable to the disarray of the previous regime.

Dean Coombe was a tall lean man in his forties, heavily whiskered, as was the fashion in those days, and of High Church leanings. He was in possession of a wife and a daughter, almost as angular as he was. He was an upright man, but stiff and overbearing; he inspired respect perhaps, but no great affection. Being active and zealous in all his dealings, he very soon began to turn his attention to the fabric of Morchester Cathedral which was indeed in a woeful state of disrepair.

The tenure of Dean Ainsley had been marked by neglect towards the great building he was appointed to maintain, so it was perhaps only just that this legacy of dereliction should be mitigated by his posthumous one. The late Dean had left his entire and considerable fortune to the cathedral, with the provision that a chapel, dedicated to the Virgin Mary, in the north transept should be made as a permanent memorial to him. As the legacy more than amply provided for this, it was resolved, by the Dean and Chapter, to accept it. There had been murmurings from some of the more Low Church canons that the building of a Lady Chapel might give rise to accusations of popery, but these were properly dismissed as old fashioned. The Dean was a forceful man and was used to carrying all before him.

An architect was engaged and there needed only a decision

to be made over the location of the chapel. The obvious place was an area closest to the crossing and facing east. This would entail the partial destruction of the eastern wall of the north transept, an exercise which would require the relocation of a number of funereal plaques and stones, the most significant of which was a sixteenth century memorial to a Canon of Morchester Cathedral, one Jeremiah Staveley. It was quite an elaborate affair in polished black basalt about five foot in height, set into the wall some three feet above the ground. It consisted of a slab topped with scrollwork, crudely classical in feel with a niche in which was set a painted alabaster image of the Canon, standing upright in his clerical robes with his arms crossed over his chest. The figure was tall and narrow, the bearded face gaunt: a somewhat disconcerting image which looked as if it portrayed the corpse rather than the living being. Beneath this on the polished slab an inscription had been incised, the lettering picked out in white. It read:

JEREMIAH STAVELEY *Canonus Morcastriensis, obiit anno 1595 aetat 52*

It was followed by these verses in bold capital letters:

BEHINDE THESE SACRED STONES IN DEATH STAND I

FOR THAT IN LIFE MOST BASELY DID I LIE

IN WORD AND SINNE FORSAKING GOD HIS LAWE,

I DANCED MY SOULE IN SATANN'S VERIE MAWE.

WHEREFORE IN PENANCE I THIS VIGILL KEEPE

ENTOMBÉD UPRIGHT THUS WHERE I SHOULDE SLEEPE.

WHEN DEAD RISE UP I'LL READYE BE IN PLACE

TO MEET MY JUDGE AND MAKER FACE TO FACE.

STRANGER, REST NOT MY CORSE UNTIL THAT DAYE

LEST I TORMENT THEE WITH MY SORE DISMAYE.

The implication of these lines, that the body of Canon Staveley was actually entombed behind the slab, was borne out by the Cathedral records and one of the old vergers whose family had been connected with the cathedral since time immemorial. Dean Coombe was disposed to be rather benevolent towards this worthy whose name was Wilby. The man was a repository of cathedral history and lore and the Dean was content to listen politely to Wilby's ramblings, but he did not expect his condescension to be rewarded by opposition to his plans.

"Mr Dean," said Wilby one afternoon, as they stood before the memorial in the north transept. "You don't want to go a moving of that there stone, begging your pardon, sir."

"My dear man, why ever not?"

"Don't it say so plain as brass on that there 'scription? 'Tis ill luck to move the bones of the wicked. So said my granfer, and his before him."

"And who says this Canon Staveley was a wicked man?"

"Why 'tis well known. There are tales that have passed down about Jeremiah Staveley, which I might blush to tell you, Mr Dean. The poor women of this city were not safe in their beds from him, they say. A harsh man too, to those below him. But he was a fair man of music and when I were a lad in the choir they still sang his setting to the Psalm one hundred and thirty-seven. 'By the waters of Babylon …', all nine verses too. With the dashing of children agin the stones and all. Some said he would have fain dinged his choir lads agin the stones, too, when they were singing awry. Certain it was, he spared not the rod among them. And there were tales of meeting at night in the church with a man all in black, and a gold treasure that he found under the earth in a field that the black man took him to. But it weren't no good for him, for soon as he was by way of enjoying his gold, the plague fell on him and he wasted to a wraith of skin and bone, and him as tall and narrow as may be already. And when at last he came to be in extreme, as you say, and within a hand's breadth of mortality, he summons the Dean, as it might be you, sir, a man with whom he had had some mighty quarrel, and begs him for forgiveness and to be shriven of his many sins. And all his treasure they say he left to the Dean and Chapter but saying he must be buried upright, to keep him awake, he says. Because in the last days he suffered terribly from dreams and was as mortally afeared of sleep as he was of death. So he begged to be buried upright that he might not sleep till the Last Judgement, even as a dead man. And when the Dean of that time, Dean Cantwell, as I think it was, came out from seeing Canon Staveley on his deathbed, they say the Dean's face was as white as a linen altar cloth and he spoke not a word to a mortal soul for seven days. This I had from my granfer who had it from his, and it came down in the family with a warning, as my old father used to say. 'Don't you touch the Staveley stone, nor go nigh it at night, nor suffer his bones to be moved.' And that's what I say to you, begging your pardon, Mr Dean."

"Well, well, Wilby," said Dean Coombe who was rather more shaken by this recitation than he cared to admit, "that is indeed a most fascinating legend. Most interesting. I must write some of it down."

"It weren't no legend, Mr Dean," said old Wilby. "I had it from my granfer, and he—"

"Quite so, quite so, my dear man," said the Dean hurriedly. "Nevertheless, move this old monument we must. But make no mistake, we shall resite it well, for it is certainly a curiosity, and if there are any human remains behind it we shall lay them to rest with all due respect. Goodness me! What was that noise?"

Both Wilby and Dean Coombe heard it, a sound like a long inhalation of breath, ragged and rattling, somewhat as if the breather – if such there was – was experiencing difficulty in drawing in air. It was magnified and distorted by the cathedral's echo which was particularly reverberant in that part of the building. Dean Coombe was not a fanciful man but he had been at his father's deathbed and he knew the sound of a man's breathing as he nears the end. This sound was uncomfortably like it.

"Dear me," said the Dean. "I really must have that organ

9

seen to."

Wilby gave the Dean a quizzical stare, then, bidding him a hurried "Good day, Mr Dean" he began to shuffle off in the direction of the West Door with surprising swiftness. Dean Coombe remained behind, standing before the monument. A passer-by was surprised to hear him mutter.

"Hah! You won't affright me that easy, Master Staveley. We shall see!"

The following day, the workmen moved in and began the demolition of the eastern wall of the north transept. Dean Coombe had given explicit instructions that the memorial slabs were to be most carefully removed, and, towards evening, he was on hand when the dismantling of the Staveley Memorial began. Palmer, the head mason, had set up scaffolding and constructed a wooden cradle in which to take the stone.

Dean Coombe suggested that the painted alabaster effigy in the niche be removed first, but this proved unexpectedly troublesome. The statue had been very securely cemented to its base, and one of the workmen cut himself on one of the folds of the statue's long gown. The workmanship was unusually precise and unworn by time.

When the effigy was finally removed, Dean Coombe was intrigued to find that it had been carved all round and that the back of the figure, which had been unseen by any living soul since it had been placed in the niche over two hundred and fifty years ago, had been carved with as much care as the visible front. He noted with particular interest the minuteness with which the sculptor had represented every snaking strand of the subject's unusually long black hair. He had also taken care to represent a gold seal ring on the third finger of the left hand, even incising the seal with a strange geometrical figure.

The face too repaid closer inspection. As Dean Coombe remarked to a colleague the following day, in a rather striking phrase, it would seem to have been "done from the death rather than from life." The skin had been painted white, with a slight yellow tinge, the cheeks were sunken and gaunt and – a rather troubling detail – the mouth gaped slightly, revealing a tiny set of jagged greenish teeth. Then there were the eyes.

Dean Coombe did not care to dwell long on the eyes. There was, as he later remarked, something "not quite dead" about them. Under the heavy lids an area of creamy white showed punctuated by the pinpoint of a pupil in a cloudy, greyish iris. The impression given was of a last wild stare at life. The painter of the statue had somehow managed to convey the terror of the sinner at the very point of death.

Despite a certain distaste (as he chose to call it) Dean Coombe was impressed by the remarkably fine workmanship of the image. In the few moments of leisure that he allowed himself he was something of an antiquarian which was why one of his many projects for the Cathedral was the setting up of a museum in the chapter house where some of the old plate and vestments of the cathedral could be displayed for the benefit of both the public and the cathedral which would take its sixpences.

"This is such fine work," said the Dean, in reality thinking aloud, but ostensibly addressing Palmer the mason. "I wonder if the craftsmanship could be Spanish, though they tended to carve in wood rather than alabaster. Certainly whoever did the painting, not necessarily the sculptor, for the painting of sculpture was a specialised art in those days, you know, looks to have been trained in the peninsular. Most unusual. I must get up something to one of the learned journals on the subject. Now then, Palmer, I want you to set this aside. Take great care of it. I shall have a plaster copy made. The replica we will put back in the niche and we can display the original in my chapter house museum, in a glass case where it may be appreciated from all angles— Good gracious, what was that?"

There had been a cry of pain accompanied by – had it been an oath? Palmer and the Dean looked around much startled as they had been absorbed in the contemplation of the effigy. However they soon discovered the cause: it was one of the workmen who had accidentally dropped a lump hammer on his foot. He was much rebuked both by Palmer for carelessness and by Dean Coombe for making an unseemly noise in a sacred building. The man protested that some mysterious force had knocked the hammer from his hand, but he was not listened to, for by this time the light was dimming and it was decided to abandon work for the day.

And so Dean Coombe began to make his way home to the Deanery across the darkling close on that cool March evening. Picture him if you will as he takes this journey, a man you might say not much given to strange fears and frets. Here is a man who walks in life both inwardly and outwardly straight ahead, looking neither to left nor right, untroubled by fancy. This is what you would have said had you seen him stride out from the West Door to face a sun which was falling behind the ancient elms in an untidy wrack of clouds. Now he turns a little to his left, and sets forth diagonally across the grass to where the Deanery is situated at the south-west corner of the great close which surrounds the edifice of St Anselm's, Morchester.

Barely has he begun on this journey when a whole crowd of rooks, a 'building' of them, if I may use the correct ornithological term, rises as one from the elms and begins to wheel about above the trees uttering their distinctive "kaa, kaa" sound. Dean Coombe must have witnessed this behaviour countless times, and yet he starts and pauses for a moment to consider those birds. Their flappings across the ensanguined sky of evening appear to him more than usually agitated and chaotic, and their strange, forlorn cries, more desolate even than normal. But these thoughts occupy him for no longer than a few seconds, and then he is on his way once more.

He quickens his pace, now more resolved than ever to reach his destination. Yet once or twice we see him glance quickly behind him, so quickly that one wonders if he truly wants to see if anything follows. By the time he reaches the gate of the Deanery passers-by are amazed to see that this very sober divine is almost running. The housemaid is equally astonished to open the door to a breathless man.

Quieta Non Movere

We will pass over the Dean's next few hours. Let us say only that the Deanery, though spacious, is a chilly, damp old house, rather too near the river for comfort. Its physical atmosphere, moreover, is matched by that which exists among its inhabitants. Relations between the Dean and his wife have become distant over the years, and his daughter is a silent creature who longs to escape the Deanery but possesses neither the youth, nor the looks, nor the accomplishments to do so.

After dinner the Dean spends some time in his study before retiring to bed writing letters and making notes for the forthcoming chapter meeting. His wife passes by his study door twice bearing an oil lamp. She has taken to these nocturnal perambulations lately because she cannot sleep. On the second occasion, it being close on midnight, she looks in to remind her husband of the fact and finds him not writing, but staring dully at the dying embers of his fire. When he becomes aware of her presence he starts violently and stares at her as if she were a stranger. Coolly Mrs Coombe reminds him of the hour, a remark which he dismisses with a perfunctory: "Thank you, my dear." Soon afterwards she hears his heavy tread on the stairs as he goes to his bedroom.

Unlike his wife, Dean Coombe is accustomed to sleeping soundly, and it is one of the reasons why they sleep apart. She would plague him far into the night with troublesome questions and admonitions if they still shared a bed. She has acquired a habit of discontent of late and he lacks the imagination to supply the remedy.

His own bedroom is small, for Mrs Coombe occupies the official matrimonial chamber, but it has a fine view over the close, and from the bed, if the curtains are open, you may just see the western front of St Anselm's. Dean Coombe does not close the curtains because he likes to imagine himself the guardian of this great edifice, keeping watch over it by day and night.

Once his nightshirt is on, the Dean feels suddenly exhausted, but still he kneels dutifully by the bed to say his prayers. But

13

when he has climbed into bed he falls almost immediately into a heavy sleep from which two hours later he is awakened with almost equal suddenness.

The moon is up and shines across his bedchamber with a clear cold light. Coombe thinks he has been awakened by a noise, but all is silence. Then he hears a sound. It is like wings fluttering in a confined space, a bird trapped in a box perhaps, but he cannot tell whether it comes from within the room or just outside the window. He chooses to believe the latter and sits up in bed to see out. There is not a cloud in the sky and the pitiless stars are out. The west front of the cathedral, whose details he can barely make out, looks to him like a hunched old man in rags, the dark rents in his clothing formed by the windows and niches of its elaborate facade. He is invaded by a feeling of infinite solitude, and in the silence that follows his ears become increasingly alert to any noise, but none comes. The stillness now seems to him unnatural.

As he continues to stare at the view beyond the window, screwing and unscrewing his eyes to get a better sight of it, he begins to be troubled by what he is looking at. For some moments he tries to find a rational explanation. At length his eyes become concentrated upon a dark bump or lump at the bottom of the window and beyond the glass. It looks to him as if he is staring at the top of a man's head, the greater part of which is below the window. He even thinks he can make out a few wayward strands of hair upon it.

"Nonsense!" He says to himself several times. "Ridiculous! Impossible!" But the fancy does not leave him. Then the head begins to move and lift itself up, as if to look at him.

With a great cry, Coombe leaps out of bed and dashes to the window in time to see a rook, which had been perched on the sill, flap away towards its building among the elms. It was only a rook! But then, rooks are not in the habit of perching on window-sills at dead of night.

Nothing more happened to the Dean that night, but he did not sleep. At breakfast the following morning his wife noted

14

how pale and drawn he looked, but she offered no solicitude. That would have been to break the barrier that had arisen between them, and she could not do that. She felt safer behind it. The Dean would have been glad of some comfort, but he, like her, had passed the point of being able to ask for it.

That afternoon in the Cathedral, Dean Coombe was present when Palmer and his men began to ease away the memorial slab to Jeremiah Staveley. All had been prepared for the possibility of human remains being found in a recess behind the stone, but no one had anticipated the smell. As the slab supported by ropes, came slowly away to be laid on a specially constructed wooden cradle, an overpowering odour pervaded not only the north transept but the whole cathedral. The organist stopped playing and several of the workmen took their hands off the stone slab to put handkerchiefs up to their noses. For a moment the memorial stone swung free on its ropes and threatened to crash into the wall and break into fragments, but just in time Palmer called his men to order and the object was laid to rest in its cradle on the scaffolding.

For almost half a minute after this had happened, nothing could be heard in that great cathedral but the sound of coughing and retching. One of the apprentice boys was violently ill into the font. Those who recalled the incident to me describe the odour as being one of mould, more vegetable than animal, "like," as one told me, "a heap of decaying cucumbers in a damp cellar." Others offered different similes, but all agreed that the scent stayed with them, on their clothes and in their nostrils for several days. Another told me that from that day forward he could never so much as look at a ripe cheese without feeling ill.

It was a while therefore before those present could bear to look at what the removal of the slab had revealed. When they did, they found themselves looking at a figure that strikingly resembled the painted alabaster effigy which had been removed the previous day.

It was the body of a man in a black clerical gown with his

15

arms crossed over his chest. The skin was still present, but dark yellow, leathery and stretched tightly over the bones. The eyes had fallen into the skull, the nose was somewhat flattened, but otherwise the face was in a remarkable state of preservation. As with the alabaster effigy, the mouth gaped slightly to reveal a set of jagged and discoloured teeth. The hair and beard were an intense and almost lustrous black. Even the nails were still present on the digits of the skeletal hands and feet. A seal ring on the third finger of the left hand was of bright, untarnished gold incised with an unusually elaborate geometrical figure.

In silence the company wondered at this strange vision, and it occurred to several of them that it was astonishing that the corpse still remained upright. Then, as they looked, the body began to collapse and disintegrate before their eyes. The first thing to go was the lower jaw, which fell off the face and shattered into a thousand dusty fragments on the cathedral floor. Then, almost like a living thing, the corpse buckled at the knees, lurched slightly forward and plunged to the ground from its recess. A dreary sound, half way between a rattle and a sigh, accompanied this final dissolution.

It was a shocking moment, but the Dean was the first to recover from it. He commanded that the remains should be gathered up and placed in the long deal box which had been provided for the purpose.

While this was being done, the Dean suddenly uttered a sharp: "No you don't, young man!" and sprang upon one of the apprentices who had been putting Canon Staveley's bones into the box. Dean Coombe thrust his hand into one of the boy's pockets and brought out a bright, golden object. It was Staveley's seal ring.

When I interviewed that boy ten years later, he was by then a most respectable young man, and the owner of a thriving building business in Morchester. He told me honestly that he had intended to steal the ring and sell it to buy medicine for his sick mother. Nevertheless, he said, he came to be very glad that he had been caught out in the theft. He also told me that Dean Coombe had not returned the ring to the deal box but had placed it in his waistcoat pocket, muttering something about "the cathedral museum." I can testify that there is no sixteenth century seal ring among the antiquities on display in the Morchester Cathedral Museum.

When he left the cathedral later that day Dean Coombe seemed in more than usually good spirits. So we will leave him for a moment and return to the young apprentice whom I have mentioned. His name was Unsworth and he told me that Palmer, the head mason, a strict but fair man, had spoken to him sharply about the attempted theft, but knowing his situation with a sick mother and no father, said he would not dismiss him. Nevertheless, as a punishment, he made the boy stay on in the cathedral to sweep and tidy up after the other workmen had gone. Never, Unsworth told me, had he performed a task with greater reluctance.

If there had not been a verger or somebody about – Unsworth heard footsteps occasionally and some fragments of dry, muttered conversation – the boy might have fled the scene and braved the consequences. As it was, he did his work conscientiously in spite of the smell which was still all-pervasive.

One of his last tasks was to nail down the lid of the deal box which held the remains of Canon Staveley. Before the body was hidden forever from public gaze Unsworth felt a compulsion to take a last look at the corpse. Much of it had turned to dust but parts of the skull and the long thin limbs were intact with shreds of parchment skin still clinging to the bone. Curiously, the black gown in which Staveley was clothed had suffered even more than the body from exposure to the air. It was now in rags and tatters, no longer recognisable as a cassock.

Unsworth covered the deal box with the lid and banged in the nails with a hammer to secure it. With each blow of the hammer Unsworth fancied he heard a cry, distant, perhaps coming from a dog or a cat outside the cathedral. He finished his work with reckless speed.

As he left the cathedral, Unsworth told me, some sort of choir practice was in progress. He remembers the groan of the organ and a piercingly high treble voice singing in a style that was unfamiliar to him. Nevertheless he remembered the words because he knew that they came from the end of the 137th Psalm:

"Happy shall he be that taketh thy children and dasheth them against the stones."

As he stepped outside the cathedral, Unsworth saw that the sun was low on the horizon sinking through a yellow sky dappled with purple cloudlets. He breathed the untainted evening air with relief. There were not many people about in the close and the noise of the day was hushed. The rooks had settled into their nests in the elms. It was a still evening with very little wind, perhaps even a trifle oppressive.

Unsworth had come out of the west door of the cathedral, the only one open at that time of day, but his home lay to the east of it. His quickest route home took him around the northern side of the Cathedral with the setting sun behind him. Unsworth remembers feeling a vague sense of apprehension as he set off.

Along the northern side of the close were a few private dwellings and a long low stretch of almshouses occupied by the poor pensioners of the diocese. Unsworth could see a few of their windows dimly glowing. In front of these almshouses were little gardens bordered by a low stone wall with gates in them for each dwelling. Most of these gates were wooden and painted white, which showed up against the grey stone houses and the deepening violet of the northern sky. As he rounded the north transept of the cathedral Unsworth had to pass quite near to these gates and it was then that he saw a human figure silhouetted against one of them.

He took the figure to be that of a man because he could see the legs which were unnaturally long and thin, almost stick-like

18

in appearance. The arms were similarly emaciated and the head narrow and oblong. He could not see any clothes on the creature except for a few black rags which fluttered faintly in the mild evening breeze.

He did not care to look too closely, but he took it to be some drunken vagrant, not simply because of the rags but because of the way it moved. It was swaying uneasily from side to side and waving its arms about. Unsworth told me that he was reminded of some long-legged insect, perhaps a spider, that has become stuck in a pool of jam and is making frantic efforts to escape from its entrapment. The thinness of those writhing legs and arms appalled him.

Unsworth started to run, but was brought up short by the sound of a cry. It was perfectly expressive, but so high above a human pitch that it resembled a dog whistle. It pierced his brain and stopped him from moving. The noise spoke to him of desolation and rage, like that of a child that has been left to scream in its cot, except that the cry was even more shrill and had no innocence to it. It was the shrieking fury of an old, old man. Unsworth found that his legs could not move. Looking behind him he saw that the stick creature had begun to stagger stiffly towards him, still uncertain on its feet, but with growing confidence.

A succession of little screams accompanied these staggering steps which seemed to indicate that movement was causing it pain, but that it was determined to stir. With its long attenuated legs it began to make strides towards him. It was coming on, but still Unsworth told me, he could not stir, "like in those dreams, sir," he said, "when you want to fly but cannot."

Suddenly the great bell of the cathedral boomed out the hour of seven and Unsworth was released from his paralysis. He ran and ran until he reached the gatehouse at the eastern end of the close where he stopped for breath and looked back. The creature was no longer coming towards him. He could see its starved outline clearly against the last of the setting sun. It had turned south-west and with long, slightly staggering strides was

19

making its way, as Unsworth thought, towards the Deanery.

Let us now go there ourselves before whatever it was that Unsworth saw arrives.

Dean Coombe sups, as usual, with his wife and daughter. Conversation, even by Deanery standards, is not lively during this meal. It is plain to Mrs Coombe and her daughter Leonora that their master is preoccupied and anxious to escape from them to his study. Perhaps he has a sermon to write, thinks Mrs Coombe idly, half remembering a time when she interested herself passionately in his doings. Even the fact that her husband seems quite indifferent to her company no longer troubles her.

The Dean has barely taken his last mouthful when, with a muttered apology, he wipes his mouth with his napkin and excuses himself from the table. A few minutes later we find him in his study. A fire is glowing in the grate and an oil lamp illumines the desk on which it has been placed. Outside the uncurtained window dusk is falling rapidly over the cathedral close.

The Dean begins to take several volumes down from his shelves. One of those he needs is on the very topmost shelf, and to obtain it he makes use of a set of library steps. He plucks the book from its eyrie and, for some moments he leafs through it rapidly on the top of the steps until we hear a little sigh of satisfaction. He descends the steps with his book, which he places beneath the lamp on his desk. The work is Barrett's *Magus* and the page at which it is open has many sigils and diagrams printed on it. The Dean now takes the gold seal ring from his waistcoat pocket and begins to compare the design incised upon it with those in the book.

There is a rap at the door. The Dean looks up sharply and plunges the golden ring back into his pocket.

"Yes!" He says in a voice, half irritable, half fearful.

The door opens. It is his wife. She says: "Stephen, did you hear that dreadful noise just now?"

"What noise, my dear?"

20

"A sort of shrieking sound. From the close. Do you think it is those boys from the workhouse making a nuisance of themselves again? Hadn't you better see what is going on?"

"My dear, I heard nothing. Are you sure it wasn't a bird of some kind?"

"No, of course, it wasn't a bird. It was nothing like a bird. I would have said if it was a bird. Are you sure you heard nothing?"

"Quite sure, my dear," says Dean Coombe in his mildest voice, though inwardly he seethes with impatience. The truth is, he *has* heard something, but he does not want to prolong the conversation with his wife. Mrs Coombe expresses her incredulity with a pronounced sniff and leaves the room, shutting the door in a marked manner.

As soon as she has gone, the Dean has taken the ring from his pocket once again and begins to pore over the designs in the book. So intent is he on his studies that at first he really does not hear the odd crackling noise that begins to manifest itself outside his window. It is a sound like the snapping of dry twigs. Slowly however, he becomes vaguely aware of some mild irritant assaulting the outer reaches of his consciousness, but he applies himself all the more ferociously to his research. Then something taps on his window.

Startled he looks up. What was it? The beak of a bird? There it is again! No, it is not a bird. Some sort of twig-like object or objects were rattling against the pane. Perhaps his wife had been right and it was those wretched workhouse boys up to their pranks. Dean Coombe goes to the window and opens it.

It was at this moment that a Mrs Meggs happened to be passing the Deanery. She was the wife of a local corn merchant and a woman of irreproachable respectability. I had the good fortune to interview her at some length about what she saw that evening, and, after some initial reluctance, she proved to be a most conscientious witness.

Despite the gathering dusk, she told me, there was still light enough to see by. What she saw first was something crouching

21

in the flower bed below the window of the Dean's study. It appeared to be a man in rags, "though 'twas all skin and bone, and more like a scarecrow than a living being," she told me. The man's hands were raised above his head, and with his immensely long and narrow fingers he appeared to be rattling on the Dean's window. Then Mrs Meggs saw the Dean open the window and look out, "very cross in the face," as she put it. Immediately the figure that had been crouched below the window-sill reared up and appeared to embrace the Dean with its long thin arms. It might have looked like a gesture of affection except that for a moment Mrs Meggs saw the expression on Dean Coombe's face which, she said, was one of "mortal terror".

"Next moment," Mrs Meggs told me, "the thin fellow in rags had launched himself through the window after the Dean and I heard a crash inside. Then I heard some shouting and some words, not distinct, but I do remember hearing the Dean cry out. 'God curse you, take your ring back, you fiend!' And I remember thinking such were not the words that should be uttered by a Man of God, as you might say. Then comes another crashing, and a cry such as I never hope to hear again as long as I live. It was agony and terror all in one. Well, by this time I was got to the door of the Deanery and banging on it with my umbrella for dear life. The maid lets me in, all of a flutter, and when we come to the Dean's study, Mrs Dean and Miss Leonora, the Dean's daughter, were there already, and Miss Leonora screaming fit to wake the dead. And who could blame her, poor mite? For I saw the Dean and he was all stretched back in his chair, his head twisted, and his mouth open and black blood coming out of it. There was no expression in the eyes, for he had no eyes, but only black and scorched holes as if two burning twigs had been thrust into their sockets."

Only one thing remains to tell. At the Dean's funeral in the cathedral some weeks later it was noticed that, though the widow was present, Dean Coombe's daughter, Leonora was not. However, as the congregation were leaving the cathedral after the service, they heard a cry in the air above them. Looking up they saw a tiny figure on the south tower of the west front. It appeared to be that of a woman waving her arms in the air. Some of the more sharp sighted among the crowd recognised the figure as that of Miss Leonora Coombe.

In horrified impotence they watched as Leonora mounted the battlements of the tower and hurled herself off it onto the flagstone path at the base of the cathedral. Her skirts billowed out during the fall but did nothing to break it, and, as she descended all the rooks in the elms of the close seemed to rise as one and set up their hoarse cries of "kaa, kaa, kaa."

When Leonora hit the ground her head was shattered, and the only mercy of it was that she had died instantly.

Later, in recalling this final episode of the tragedy, several witnesses quoted to me, as if compelled by some inner voice, those final words of the 137th psalm:

"Happy shall he be that taketh thy children and dasheth them against the stones."

THE LAST COACH TRIP

David A. Riley

Hamer Street Working Men's Club had been in decline for more years than Harold cared to remember. Built around the time of Victoria's death, it had managed to thrive through two world wars, the Depression, strikes, the three-day week, the advent of cinema, radio, even TV, right up until the 1980s. After that a kind of acceleration seemed to set in with cheap beer from supermarkets and the attraction of videos, then DVDs, and its days became numbered. The cigarette ban was the final blow, Harold was sure. Now in his seventies he was sad to think that in a few weeks a way of life he had grown to love would end when the club closed its doors for good.

"At least it'll go with a bang." Eddie nudged him as if he'd read his thoughts. Not that this would have been difficult. The club's closure had dominated their talk for months.

Harold sighed. Tipping the last of his beer into his mouth, he struggled to his feet; sciatica niggled the base of his spine. "Another?" he asked unnecessarily before trudging to the bar.

The main part of the club was a large rectangular room, a cluster of tables and chairs close to the bar, a padded couch down the longest wall by a snooker table, with one-armed bandits near the door. These gave the club what profit it made, since its members had long ago made it clear they weren't in favour of paying more than they had to do for their beer, already the cheapest in Edgebottom. Not that this had done much to sustain membership. Perhaps nicotine-coloured walls and foul-smelling toilets had much to do with it, plus no TV, vetoed by the committee whenever the subject was raised.

Harold enjoyed its exclusivity. Its members were mostly working class men, retired these days, who came here to drink, exchange some gossip and air what wisdom they had about world events with lifelong friends, and perhaps play dominoes, sometimes for money.

"Quiet tonight," Eddie said when he returned with their pints.

"A lot of them'll be saving for the trip." As would he, Harold thought, if he hadn't a bit put to one side in the bank. His pension wouldn't have paid for his nightly visits to the club *and* the trip, not nowadays.

"The last coach trip," Eddie said with disbelieving reverence. "Who'd have thought it?"

"Aye." Harold shook his head, then tasted his beer. Satisfied, he gulped a quarter down, then relaxed, feeling sad. "We should make the most of it," he said. "In a few weeks all we'll have left will be memories."

"I've too many o' them already." Though a couple of years younger than Harold, Eddie had always looked older, his face furrowed with wrinkles down both cheeks. "Still," he said, with a smile that nudged these into curves around dentures too perfect to be real, "the trip'll be a stylish way to end it."

The club's coach trip to Ripon Races had been an annual event for as long as Harold could remember. It was an all male affair that started in the morning with pints at the club till the coach turned up, breakfast at a country pub, then an afternoon of gambling on the nags before a slap-up meal en route to a Yorkshire nightclub and their eventual return to Edgebottom in the wee hours of the morning. Last year, Harold had won over fifty pounds from the bookies, though most of it went on drink that night – and one of the worst hangovers he'd had for years. Still, it had been worth it. It always was.

"There aren't as many of us this year," Eddie said. "There was talk of getting a minibus instead of a coach. They'd have done it too, but there are too many of us."

"It wouldn't be the same in one of those bloody things. We need a full size coach with plenty o' legroom."

"Like I said, we're going out in style."

Harold grunted. "You make it sound as if we're snuffing it."

Eddie shook his head. "Feels like it sometimes," he said. "The end of an era."

The Last Coach Trip

Harold glanced at his friend. He was even more sombre than usual tonight. "You could do with something to cheer you up." Harold reached in his pocket, counting his change. "Here – I'll get us a round of Glenfiddich. That'll do the trick."

*

It didn't seem long before the weeks passed and Harold was sitting at his usual spot a yard from the bar, waiting for the coach to arrive. He'd arrived early wearing his Sunday best. Feeling lucky today, he'd drawn a few extra pounds from the bank and was going to have the kind of afternoon with the bookies he'd only ever dreamed about in previous years, going out in style, as Eddie said. He worried about Eddie. He had become more morose over the last few weeks. He'd lost weight too, though he'd never had much meat on his bones. The club's pending closure had seemed to depress him even more than the rest of the regulars. Not that any of them were jumping around with joy. Harold was too old to start going into pubs again. Apart from their trip to the races, he had only ever drunk in the club for years. And from what he'd heard he'd missed nothing. Revamped, their insides gutted, most pubs had been turned into drinking holes for snotty-nosed youngsters out to get pissed or been turned into licensed restaurants. The old-fashioned backstreet pub was a thing of the past. Like workingmen's clubs, he thought. Harold shook his head. He would probably end up drinking cans of beer in front of the telly, something he had never done before in his life except at Christmas. Alice would turn in her grave at the thought.

Harold glanced at his watch. It was time Eddie was here. Growing concerned, Harold glanced around the club. Despite the smoking ban there was a haze around the bar. Big Bill Entwhistle and his chums were leant against it, puffing away at cigars. No doubt they were going to finish in style too, Harold thought as he glanced around the faces of those who were here.

Only Eddie was missing. Which was worrying. Eddie was never late for anything. Ever.

Grimacing at the ache in his back, Harold pushed himself to his feet. He gulped down the last of his beer before wandering to the door. As always it felt strange to be looking out onto the cobblestone street at this time of day. A few more minutes and the coach would be here. Harold stepped outside and looked up the street towards Eddie's house, but the only figure was a paperboy burdened with an oversized bag. Come on, Harold thought, agitated now. They had talked so much about today he couldn't believe that Eddie was late. They had left the club early last night so they would both be fresh this morning.

"Where's Eddie got to?" It was Frank White, another veteran of more than forty-year's membership. He rubbed the bristly nostrils of his nose and peered outside, squinting as if sunlight hurt his eyes. Broken veins trailed across cheeks the colour of weathered putty.

Harold shrugged, unwilling to think what might have delayed his friend, but knowing it had to be serious.

"You don't think he's ill?" Frank stared at him with too much concern for Harold's taste. He didn't want to think down those lines yet.

"There's time. Coach isn't due till eight-thirty."

"He's cutting it fine. Driver won't want to hang around. He's a schedule to keep."

"He'll hang around if he has to," Harold said. "Eddie's paid his dues like everyone else."

"Everyone else is here."

Harold shook his head. "He's not late yet."

"Too late for a pint afore we set off." Frank beamed with triumph. "First time he's missed in thirty year."

Harold was tempted to go to the bar and order Eddie a pint to wipe the smirk off Frank's face, but it would be petty – and pointless. If Eddie wasn't here by now he more than likely wouldn't be here at all. Deep down Harold knew this. He wondered if he should go to Eddie's house to find out what

27

was wrong. Stubbornly, Eddie still hadn't had his phone reconnected two years after it was cut off. "If I can't pay for it now how the 'ell do you think I'll manage in future?" he said when Harold tackled him about it. Harold told him he was being pig-headed, that you never knew when you might need a phone in an emergency. Harold hoped there hadn't been one today, though he knew nothing less could have kept his friend from being here.

There was a rumble as the coach arrived outside. Hydraulic brakes hissed as it stopped beside the club.

Too late, Harold thought as the coach's shadow loomed inside the club through its dappled windows. He glanced at his watch, then hurried outside. "Driver, wait a few minutes, will you? I'm going to see what's held up my friend. He should have been here by now."

"I am," a voice behind him said.

Shocked, Harold spun round, twisting his hip. He felt a chill down his spine.

"You daft bugger. D'you want to give me a heart attack?"

Eddie grinned. "I got here as quick as I could. I overlaid."

And looked it. Chalky stubble showed that he hadn't even shaved. Or put on a tie, Harold realised, though Eddie was never seen without one. "If you were thirty years younger I'd be asking where you'd spent the night."

"Thirty?" Frank said, waddling over. "More like fifty. What you been up to, Eddie? Birding it?"

Eyeing the liverish look on his friend's face, Harold said, "Leave him alone. He's here, isn't he?"

"So long as he isn't sick when we set off."

Frank walked away, laughing.

"Take no notice of the sarcastic bastard," Harold said.

"Never have." Eddie leaned against the outside wall.

"Are you all right?" Harold asked. "You don't look so clever."

"Felt better." Eddie took a deep breath. It wheezed down his throat, disturbingly deep.

28

"Do you want to give the trip a miss? See the doctor? I'll go with you."

Eddie laughed. "I wouldn't ask that of you, Harold. I don't want to miss it either. There won't be no more, you know."

Harold helped him up the steps into the coach while the club steward and several committeemen loaded boxes of sandwiches and crates of beer into the boot.

"I think we'd better sit near the front," Harold said.

"In case I'm sick?"

"You never know. I might need to get off quick myself. Those beers I've had are weighing heavy. They might've been off."

A few minutes later the rest of the party climbed on board. Fewer than on previous trips, there were plenty of seats for everyone.

"Next stop the Farmer's Glory," the driver called as he set off. "Full English – for those who can manage it."

Eddie dozed most of the way to the pub. Harold kept an eye on him, not happy with his friend's jaundiced face. At the Farmer's Glory, though, Eddie recovered, grinning cheerfully. "I feel hungry enough to eat a horse."

"You'll have to make do with bacon and eggs."

"Hope there's a damn sight more than that on our plates," Bill Entwhistle said. He squeezed down the aisle, eager to be off. "We've been promised Full English."

Despite what he'd said, Eddie barely seemed to touch his food.

"You'd think it was the condemned man's last meal," Frank joked. He dabbed his lips with a napkin. "It's the last breakfast we'll have on trips like this," he said, his eyes mournful. "Might as well make the most of it."

Which sobered the mood.

"Cheer up," Harold said, taking a folded copy of the *Sporting Life* out of his pocket. "Let's pick some winners."

In an attempt to help lift everyone's mood, Harold managed to persuade everyone to have another round at the Farmer's

Glory before they trundled back to the coach. The weather was fine, with a brisk wind to freshen them up when they went outside, but Eddie soon began to feel dozy, the soft motions of the coach lulling him to sleep.

He woke up as they pulled into the car park of the Feathers. It was half an hour from the racecourse, but they always stopped here for lunch.

Eddie gazed around, barely interested in his beer. Taking it all in for the last time, Harold thought. It would hit him hard when it was over, when all they had left were memories, especially when the club closed too. Harold dreaded that. It was hard to accept change at their age, especially when it was something that had been a big part of their lives for decades.

"Have you picked any winners?" Harold asked, but Eddie shook his head. "That's not like you," Harold said. "You've usually filled your card by now. You're slipping." But Harold's attempts at humour seemed to have no impact. Please yourself, Harold thought, determined that his friend's mood swings weren't going to spoil his day. He had worried about Eddie catching the coach, and had looked after him as attentively as he could since then, concerned about his state of health, but it was his day too. If Eddie was determined to stay in this obtuse state of mind, so be it. There was an afternoon's gambling and drinking ahead and Harold wasn't going to miss any of it for anything.

Which he didn't, even though most of his horses failed to fulfil his hopes. At least there was the beer, and the weather stayed fine. He saw Eddie now and then, but his friend seemed to be in a world of his own, wandering aimlessly. Harold never caught sight of him with a drink or near the bookies, which seemed bizarre. What was the point of coming to the races if you weren't going to have a few bets or a pint of beer in the fresh air?

By the end of the afternoon Harold was thoroughly exhausted, teetering on the right side of drunk. Better still, his last race had come up trumps and a twenty-pound bet had

30

returned him a hundred. More than recouping what he'd lost, it cheered him up tremendously. Though he rarely if ever made a loss at the races, breaking even was almost as good a way to finish as any. So he felt as he ordered a pint at the bar and looked around the crowds to see if anyone from their coach was there. He needed someone with whom to brag about his win.

Which was when he saw Eddie.

Like a lost soul drifting amongst the crowds.

"Eddie!"

Harold hurried after him before he was swallowed up again and took hold of Eddie's elbow.

"What have you been up to all afternoon? Have you won any bets?"

There was a worryingly detached look on his friend's face – so detached it seemed to have smoothed its wrinkles and made him look, if anything, younger, in mind at least. Which worried Harold even more. The word Alzheimer's sprang unbidden – and he wished it hadn't. Could the club's closure in a few weeks time have brought it on? Harold didn't know enough about Alzheimer's to be sure, but he feared the worst as he stared into Eddie's eyes. There was a fey look in them. "He's been talking to the faeries," his mother would have said. It made Harold feel uneasy. Was he going to lose his closest friend as well as the club?

"Are you all right, Eddie?" he asked.

"Never felt better." Eddie smiled. It was calm and placid, a man at peace with the world. Harold doubted if Eddie had ever borne a smile like it before in his life. Scorn and cynicism, sourness and disdain, these were Eddie's usual moods, not some loopy-doopy hippy bliss as if he'd swallowed a happy pill and won first prize in the National Lottery. Harold knew then that his friend must have suffered a breakdown. That was what they called them, wasn't it? Breakdowns? He was sure it had to be the club's closure that had caused it too. A widower like Harold, it was all Eddie had left in his life. Which was a

31

bitter thing for Harold to think about. Was he any different except that he hadn't cracked up yet? Though he knew there were other ways events like this could affect men their age. Decline, loneliness, and death, these were more likely, he knew. A fine old way to end your life, he thought as he drew Eddie towards the bar. Perhaps his friend was the lucky one.

"Here, sit down and I'll fetch us a couple o' pints." Harold guided Eddie to a vacant seat in the open air not far from the bar. Like the rest, the table beside them was awash with an afternoon's spilled beer. Cigarette ash flowed through it like industrial waste.

Quieter now that most of the course's punters were beginning to head for the car park, it wasn't long before Harold returned with their drinks. He placed Eddie's down in front of him.

Eddie gazed at it, smiling benignly.

"Thanks, Harold." He didn't pick it up though.

"Bloody Hell, what's happened? Have you signed the pledge? It's for supping, not admiring. It won't get no better the longer you leave it."

As if to set an example, Harold knocked back half his pint in one swallow, though he knew he should be taking it easy now till they'd had the dinner they'd booked en route to Dewsbury. There were hours of drinking ahead of them when they got to the nightclub. If he wasn't careful he'd end up legless. It was years since he last slipped up and drank too much, though he still had a scar next to his eyes where his glasses had cut his face when he fell in the toilets of the club they'd gone to, too drunk to stand. He was taken to the local A&E to get stitched and been left to spend the rest of the night by himself in the coach till they set off home hours later. That had been a trip to remember.

Harold put down his glass. He decided to leave the rest, even if his friend did make him want to get blathered. Why did this have to happen today? Why couldn't Eddie have stayed all right till tomorrow? It wouldn't have mattered then. He knew it

32

was selfish to wish this, but it just wasn't fair. It was his last day at the races too.

"Come on, Eddie," he said, feeling guilty. "If you don't want your beer we might as well go back to the coach."

"What's up with him?" Frank asked when they'd returned to their seats. "Too much to drink?"

Harold bit back his annoyance. "He's not been feeling good all day." He glanced at Eddie's vacant gaze as he stared through the window at the passing crowds. "I don't think he's even had anything to drink."

"So you say," Frank said with a chuckle. "Looks like he's had a skinful to me."

Which was something even Harold began to suspect when they arrived at the restaurant for their evening meal. Eddie barely touched his food, even though Harold suspected he'd had nothing to eat all afternoon. He'd even refused a teacake when they stopped at the Feathers before the racecourse.

Perhaps because of all the alcohol he'd drunk, it didn't seem long to Harold before the meal was over and they were off again for the Revellers Night Club. It wasn't Harold's cup of tea, but it was part of their tradition. There was a stand-up comedian and a baby-faced crooner they were told got through to the semi-finals in last year's *The X-Factor*, though Harold didn't remember him. Not that he was bothered. The last few hours of their last coach trip were drawing to a close and, despite the drinks he'd had all day, he felt melancholic. He sat down at the table they had commandeered as far from the stage as they could get, where they could ignore the acts if they wanted to and talk instead, reminiscing over the day's events.

"Off his ale," Bill said to Harold, sotto voce. He nodded at Eddie. "Not his usual self. Last year we had to carry him to the coach." Harold remembered that night. None of them had known there'd only be one more. They'd enjoyed themselves in style that night. Really enjoyed themselves, Harold thought. Tonight was turning into a wake.

"Come on, Eddie. Liven up," Bill said.

33

Eddie looked at him and smiled. He'd smiled a lot today, Harold thought. Probably more than he'd done for the past decade. Which wasn't natural. Not for Eddie. Nor him either. Not that he'd had much to smile about except when his horse shot past the finishing line a length ahead of its nearest rival.

"Perhaps we should organise a trip of our own," Frank said. But they knew it wouldn't be the same. They'd talked about it time and again over the past few weeks, but they'd drift apart when the club shut down. It was their focal point. There was nothing to replace it.

"This is our last trip," Eddie said. He said it simply, so matter-of-factly it silenced them all for a full minute. The men exchanged glances, then slumped in their seats as the stand-up came on.

Harold felt unnaturally sober when they finally headed back to the coach at two in the morning. There was none of the usual raucous jokes or attempts at singing. He'd seen livelier funerals.

"The end of an era," Harold heard someone mutter though he couldn't tell who. It sounded resentful. Had the day been so bad? Harold rubbed his eyes, feeling old and tired. His shoulders were heavy. They weighed him down. He reached for the handrail and hoisted himself into the coach; the coldness of the air inside chilled him. It was worse than out, as if the driver had left the engine running with the air conditioning on full blast while they were in the club.

Eddie pulled himself up the steps behind him.

Fog had drawn in by the time the coach left to weave its way through the dark streets, heading for the road that would take them back to Lancashire. Dry stonewalls blurred by as they ascended Saddleworth Moor, sometimes hidden by rolls of mist that drifted towards them. Vehicle headlights were diffused through the fog, blinding one second, then gone the next. Harold didn't envy the driver his job. It had been a long day for him too and conditions were treacherous. Which probably why he sat upright at the steering wheel, stiff with

34

tension.

Harold glanced at Eddie, who was smiling to himself, contentedly.

Eddie turned and looked at him. "It's been a great day, hasn't it? A day to remember." Unexpectedly, Eddie pulled himself to his feet. He swayed unsteadily. His hands gripped the back of the seat behind the driver as the coach swung round a bend in the road.

"Driver!" Eddie's voice was discordant, loud. It drowned the hubbub of conversations in the coach behind him.

What the hell was he up to? Harold slid across the seat to stop him.

"Don't distract the driver," Harold said in a harsh whisper, but he was already too late. Startled by the tone of Eddie's voice, the driver turned. At the same time headlights flooded the windscreen.

"No!" Harold heard himself cry as if from a distance, dismay and fear paralysing him as a lorry's horn, loud as a ship's, blasted through the air.

"No what?"

Harold looked up from his beer. His eyes felt gritty when he opened them. Eddie was standing beside him, looking down.

"Are you all right?"

Harold felt befuddled. He was sitting in the club, its door wide open only a few feet away. A coach stood outside. Its windows glinted in beams of sunlight that splintered across it.

"We'll be away in a few minutes. Did you nod off?"

"I must've done." Harold's tongue felt swollen, thick when he spoke. "Jesus! I was well away," he said. He struggled to sit upright. How long had he been asleep?

"Come on." Eddie patted him on the shoulder. "We've a big day ahead of us. We need to make the most of it. It's the last we'll be having."

Eddie's voice sounded oddly cheerful. Harold turned to look round the club. Others too looked as if they must have dozed off, waiting for the coach to arrive. There was a half-awake look to most of them.

"Next stop the Farmer's Glory," the driver said as Harold clambered onto the coach a few minutes later, hauling himself up step by step, using both hands on the handrail. The driver's voice sounded lacklustre. "Full English – for those who can manage it," he ended with a stifled yawn.

Harold hoped he felt better than he looked. The driver's face seemed vacant, half-asleep, as if he'd struggled to climb out of bed this morning.

What's wrong with everyone? Only Eddie looked eager and bright. Perhaps they'd drunk too many beers on empty stomachs. It never used to bother him, but he wasn't getting any younger, he thought.

"The last coach trip," Harold murmured as the coach set off.

"You could say that," Eddie responded.

Which was when Harold found himself stumbling through half forgotten memories, of things he thought they'd already done. A hundred pound win on the last race. He could feel every greasy twenty-pound note the bookie had handed to him between his fingers. He could still taste the overdone steak he'd struggled to chew in the restaurant before they left for the Revellers. Some of the stand-up's jokes echoed through his head, corny, crude, bludgeoned by lips too close to the microphone. And the boy-like singer, crooning something sentimental, he couldn't remember what. He'd been in *The X-Factor*, hadn't he? A semi-finalist? Then the coldness of the coach when they climbed inside …

He looked at Eddie. "You weren't just late; you should never have been there."

Eddie's smile was unwavering.

"What did you do, Eddie? Kill yourself? Take an overdose?"

Which was ridiculous, he knew. The stupidest things he had ever said.

"Some days are just too good to be over," Eddie replied. "Some days should never end."

Somewhere in the back of his mind Harold remembered the pain of glass and metal hitting him, of screams as flames licked through the coach.

As he stared at Eddie his appetite for the Full English ahead of them drained away.

HOME BY THE SEA

Stephen Bacon

Look into my background and you'll find the usual catalogue of neglect and abuse. I bet you've seen the same story hundreds of times in your line of work – taken into care when I was a junior, allowed to fall through the cracks of the welfare service. By the time I was a teenager I knew how to hot-wire a car, which type of windows were the easiest to force, which shops had the weakest anti-theft devices. My life was plunged into the realms of violence and crime. It's the same old story. The only thing I managed to avoid was the pitfall of hard drugs.

Following a couple of enforced stays at Feltham, I was eventually released back onto the streets. An old mate of mine suggested I move down to Brighton with him. We slept rough for a couple of weeks before finding an abandoned lockup at the back of a row of garages. I quickly realised we were very different people from the ones that we'd been inside the Raven residential unit of the young offenders' institute. For one thing, he was a crazy bastard. How he managed to conceal this fact from the authorities, I'll never know. I caught him eating a raw blackbird one morning. At least he'd taken the trouble to pluck the bloody thing. That very same afternoon, after he'd gone to score a fix, I legged it.

I remembered years ago, when we'd been taken on a trip to the seaside from the young offenders home in Leeds. It was a bloody farce; Skinny Norris and Ally Adams ended up scrapping in one of the penny arcades, and Tony Fisher was arrested for nicking an old woman's purse from her handbag as she played bingo. The authorities threatened never to take us out again, but nonetheless my overall impression of Scarborough had been good.

The one thing I *had* remembered was a huge property that overlooked the north side of the bay. I'd studied it from one of the static telescopes that were fixed to the promenade; twenty pence for about a minute's viewing – now *that's* fucking criminal! Anyway, I assumed the massive building had been a posh hotel or one of those spa resorts that they use to fleece rich women with. I'd asked around at the fish 'n' chip shop; the bloke behind the counter said it was owned by a local bigwig, some ex-councillor or something. Anyway, the image of the potential wealth hidden beyond the facade of that old mansion got me thinking. I'd always had a soft spot for the east coast, so I decided to take a trip up north.

Scarborough retains that old-fashioned sense of nostalgia that, I suppose, still attracts people. My childhood – suppressed memories from the children's home – offered nothing warm or comforting. Unless you count the physical abuse I suffered. I wandered that first day in a haze of coloured lights and beeping machines. I managed to land a cash-in-hand job in one of the arcades. For four hours a day I would sit on a stool in the corner and hand out the paper tokens in the bingo. Winners would then exchange these tokens for the gaudy items of shitty tat that were pegged above the caller. Mostly I was dealing with pensioners and kids, so the job wasn't too taxing. And it gave me opportunity enough to research the background on the cliff-top house.

My shift ended at six o'clock each night. I'd found a bed-sit above a pizza shop, twenty minutes' walk from the sea front. The flat was greasy and smelled constantly of food. Every minute I spent in the place made me hungry.

I walked up to the road in front of the posh house one evening, and peered through the iron gates that spanned the gap in the high wall. The house languished in an expanse of grassy land, strategically landscaped to obscure the building. I made mental notes regarding the best place to climb the wall. The trees gave me plenty of cover to approach the house unseen.

Once darkness had descended on the town, I managed to get up close to the residence. It seemed quite clear that the majority of the house was unused; probably the man now lived alone, and just consigned himself to certain areas. I imagined the possibility of the treasures within, dusty heirlooms and valuable collectables that might make me a fortune in the antique shops down south.

There was a window on the house that overlooked the sea. It had an old wooden frame, in quite a poor state of repair. This, I decided, would be my point of entry.

For several days I planned my strategy. I weighed up the possibility of pulling the Opera scam. You know what I mean? You might not recognise the name, but you'll have seen that con played loads of times, I bet. It normally goes something like this –

You steal the car from the drive of an upper-class house. You know the kind I mean – a Jag or a Beamer, or a Merc. Maybe an Audi, at a push. You take it out for a spin. I mean, really put some mileage on the clock. But the thing is you have to look after the motor. No damage or anything. Then you return it later, parked in a different direction, with a thank-you note tucked under the windscreen wiper.

The next day you post a lovely letter to the address, telling the owner that you're apologising for the inconvenience you caused, but you were stuck that night and needed the use of their vehicle. As a way of compensation you enclose a couple of tickets to the theatre, for a show the following week at a nearby city. Originally the scam was the opera – hence the name – but I think the theatre works best. And then – you've guessed it – on the night in question, when the owners are out at the theatre, you've got the ideal opportunity to burgle their house, safe in the knowledge that they're otherwise occupied.

Of course, not everyone falls for it. But you tend to find the type of person who lives in these kinds of houses and drives those kinds of cars, they're not always familiar with the workings of the criminal fraternity. They're taken in by this more than you'd imagine.

Anyway, it's been years since I pulled the opera scam, but I decided to discount it. For all I could see, this house may not even be occupied. And, if I'm honest (and I've never been that!), I couldn't afford the outlay of the theatre tickets upfront, so I just plumped for the good old-fashioned breaking and entering.

So for a while I bided my time. Then, on the Thursday, the local weather report indicated there was a sea-fret due inland by the evening. I took my chance.

I hot-wired a transit van that was parked round the corner from my flat, and cautiously drove up the York road towards the entrance to the house. The mist made everything all eerie and ghost-like. Under cover of the poor visibility, I climbed the wall. I jumped down onto the lawn and looked over towards the house, but the fog was too fluid to see anything through, just vague and indistinct.

The house appeared to be in darkness. As I crossed one of the lawns towards the conservatory at the back, a security light suddenly came on. I had to duck out of sight behind a row of hedges. After a few minutes of waiting, I headed to where the wooden window was.

It was easier than I thought it would be. The screwdriver scraped out the crumbling putty and the glass was a doddle to lift out. Within minutes I was standing in a long room with a glass roof, surrounding by wicker furniture. It smelt strongly of mildew. I had brought a torch so I had to switch it on and cross to the French windows. They were unlocked so I went through into what looked like a dining room. There was a dark wooden table and loads of chairs and posh candles on the side. I took down two of the smaller paintings that were hanging on the wall and stacked them near the window.

The house was totally silent. That made me feel a bit better. It's much easier to be in and out quick if you haven't got to tiptoe around. I scoured the downstairs rooms for a while. That's where I got the two watches and the cufflinks from.

I'm not kidding, the house was just like something out of a film, all chandeliers and wooden panelling. I soon realised I'd have no need to lug any of the antique furniture out to the van – there would be riches enough with just the jewellery and the paintings. There was even a small envelope stuffed with cash, hidden in one of the drawers of the sideboard.

Somehow I'd wandered across to the other side of the house, into what I later was told was the *living quarters*. This bit looked a little more modern. There was even an old twenty-one inch television in one of the rooms. It wasn't a flat screen one though, so I decided its value meant it wasn't worth lugging back to the van.

By now I'd almost forgotten where I was; the initial rush of adrenaline you get when you first break into somewhere had faded. It was almost as if I was browsing a stately home, only instead of peering at dusty treasures and fragile ornaments I was nicking them.

Anyway, I found myself in a room at the edge of the building, overlooking the fog-shrouded bay. There was a recessed stairway cut into the wall, rising between two massive bookcases, and I headed up it.

The room above was very similar to the one I had just left, only it contained some creepy stuffed animals; a huge bird of prey gripped a struggling mouse in its claws; two glassy-eyed stags monitored the room with cold indifference; beneath a glass dome, a badger was frozen in the act of sniffing the air. There was something about the unrealistic shine of the eyes that seemed at odds with the telling detail of the animals' bodies. I'd seen things like these on car-boot sales all over the place. I didn't think the modest value warranted the care that would be required to take them.

It was just about then that I heard the splashing sound.

At first I wasn't sure what was going on. I froze, head cocked, listening with a burning intensity. The noise was barely audible, just a slight shifting in my perception. I almost *sensed* the noise, rather than heard it.

Pressing my ear to the door, I held my breath and listened. Finally I opened it. Curiously, I crept out into the corridor. A long passage extended into the distance, with doors on either side. The red carpet was faded and tired.

To my immediate right, the door was ajar. I peered through the gap and then took a sharp gasp of breath.

A small bathroom was in darkness, though pale moonlight was filtering through the frosted glass of the window. Sounds of splashing water bubbled from the toilet. I shuffled inside the small room and peered into the bowl. Something was emerging from the darkness of the U-bend.

At first I could just make out a vague bloated lump. I took a step backwards and watched in horror.

Firstly, the bulbous dome of a head squeezed out the narrow passage of porcelain as the lump emerged into the toilet bowl. The water fragmented and distorted the huge eyes and hairless face. Finally, a tiny arm extended out of the top of the bowl and grabbed the rim of the toilet seat. The fat fingers slipped slightly in the water. I stared, incredulous, at the glistening shape that pulled itself out of the toilet and flopped onto the linoleum.

It was a naked baby.

The podgy limbs twisted the body onto its hands and knees. It looked as slippery as an eel. There was a fierce intensity in its glistening face. The eyes burned from the centre of the domed bald head.

Seemingly unaware of my presence, the little thing crawled towards the open door. I watched aghast, feeling an overwhelming sense of detachment to my surroundings. Images shimmered in my vision. My stomach lurched.

The thing crawled through the doorway onto the landing, leaving a wet trail in its wake. Its movement seemed natural enough. The soft pads of the creature's feet looked perfect and unblemished.

I followed it to the threshold, where I watched it creep along the red carpet. Further along, toward the end of the corridor where the darkness gathered, something waited.

Rail-thin, pale and bruised, the young boy in football shorts and a 70s Adidas top watched with eternal patience. Behind him in the corners, where the shadows were thickest, darkness coalesced into a multitude of figures. They welcomed another of their own.

A sallow-faced girl clutched a skipping-rope; hollow sockets watched the baby's progress. Child-size skeletal figures detached from the shadows and paused, as if gathering strength. Or maybe contemplating their past.

I found myself transfixed as I watched the boy in football shorts finally turn and open the heavy door to his left.

The macabre procession filed into the room. It was truly a horrific sight; bruised limbs blurred amongst Star Wars T-shirts and Hello Kitty dresses, home-knit jumpers and bell-bottomed jeans. White skin that was so pale it was almost translucent. Clamours of energy as they ushered into the room on silent legs.

A big green leather armchair faced a writing bureau, standing against the wall. I could see that someone was sitting in it even though its back was to us.

He was really fat, this man. There was a laptop open in front of him, and random patterns vortexed round the black screen, almost as if it was mesmerising him. A glass of something-on-the-rocks stood next to the computer and the man took a gulp from it. I could smell the alcohol. His thinning hair looked greasy and thread-like.

The man suddenly seemed to sense me behind him. He turned sharply in his chair, his face washed pale from the glow of the laptop. I could see the liquid glistening on his jowls. His eyes widened in surprise as they fell on me. Then they flicked to the figures gathered in the darkness, an exhalation of shock escaping his lips.

And then, like hungry animals, the darkness swarmed over him, devouring the light until I found it difficult to see what was happening.

Two little girls eagerly clutched his head, the boy in the shorts bent quickly to tear bites from the man's neck. The crawling baby appeared to reach a podgy hand out to gouge the eyes.

I watched transfixed, unable to tear my view away, despite the atrocities I was seeing. Tiny fingers tore at the man's clothing as he struggled. Their number was too great. The light from the laptop bathed grimacing mouths, nails raking skin, bloodstained teeth gnawing at flesh.

Swathes of darkness enveloped the man. As if carried by the wind, the scream of a thousand voices burst into the room, rising in pitch until the volume hurt my ears.

I found myself propelled by the shadows, swept ahead by the eager shapes that loped or scuttled around us.

There was something about the man that disgusted me; not only the physical fat that hung from his body, but the pathetic manner in which he struggled against the fluid attack. "I'm sorry," he shrieked. "I remember you – I'm sorry." But the spindly limbs reached to silence his protests.

A howling tornado whipped into the room, buffeting me from behind but leaving everything else untouched. The gale ripped my hair and tore at my clothing. Another chorus of screams erupted, childlike and shrill in their intensity. I felt my vision juddering as I fought against the maelstrom of wind and noise. Blindly I stumbled forward, flailing in the struggle to move against the tide.

Just before I passed out, in the last moments before consciousness left me, I saw the prone body of the fat man, as the shadows and darkness feasted.

Anyway, that was the last thing I remember. The next thing I knew was waking up in the hospital with the copper at my bedside. They told me what had happened. About the fat bloke's death, I mean.

They told me to tell the truth, and that's what I've done. It might be unbelievable and I know the story is strange and you'll be suspicious of what I've said, but I'm willing to take one of them lie-detector tests to prove I'm telling the truth. The doctors have been in to see me and they've given me some drugs to help me sleep, but at night I can still see movement in the darkness; I can still imagine the pale children capering in the shadows that lurk in the corner of my cell.

I think I always will.

*

TO: Chief Superintendent William D Rogers
FROM: Detective Sergeant David Briggs
SUBJECT: Oliver Pendlebury Murder

Hi Bill,

Sorry to bother you – I know you must be busy, what with the Royal visit at the end of the month – but I just wanted to gauge your thoughts on a few points from the Pendlebury case. I'm not sure quite how I should approach the report.

I've attached the statement from the suspect, Dwayne Simmons. It's a bit of a strange one, I can tell you! There is a hint of possible schizophrenia in his words. The clarity is at odds with some passages that seem fantastic. I've also enclosed the pathologist's report. It does confirm that Pendlebury was strangled sometime on Thursday, September 18th, probably between midday and midnight.

The rest of the case looks solid. Simmons's DNA is all over the body and around the point of entry. The old bloke had external CCTV that shows the suspect entering through the window of the orangery. The bite marks on the victim's body match Simmons's dental records and the blood samples on the suspect's clothing all tie him to the murder. Looks like the sick bastard may have actually eaten parts of the old man. We shall have to tread very carefully with the press on this one.

But here comes the strange part   we've looked into Pendlebury's background a bit, and we recovered a laptop and a desktop computer from the scene that were choc-a-block with kiddy porn. The tech guys think there might be strong evidence to link him to that paedophile ring that was broken last summer. Looks like he's been up to it for years. There were even photos of himself that had been scanned on, dating back to the late 70s/early 80s. Apparently, before he moved into politics he ran a children's home in the West Midlands for many years. We're looking into the possibility that that's where Simmons knew him from, even though the kid claims he didn't know who Oliver Pendlebury was when he broke in.

There's also something peculiar in the path report. She's made a comment that there's a differential in the bite marks, almost as if they were made by loads of different people. I've tried to push her on that but she says the evidence is firm; there's a variety of wound diameters and imprints of unknown teeth formations. She suggests some of them might have been done by an animal, because the signs show such a small bite indication. I'm not sure what to make of that, if I'm honest.

Simmons himself is having psychological tests done at the moment. His statement indicates some definite evidence of mental disorder. And the fantastical nature of his report suggests we might need to go steady, from a prosecution point of view.

Let me know your thoughts once you've read the attachments, Bill. It goes without saying that the murder/child pornography/high profile of the victim aspect of the case means we have to tread very carefully.

Regards,
Dave.

BOYS WILL BE BOYS

David Williamson

The whole experience was nothing like he had imagined it would be.

Watching too many Hollywood romantic movies had lulled him into a false sense of well-being which had left him ill prepared for the grim realities of it all. He felt cheated. Cheated and sick, and not necessarily in that order, the truth be told. No, sick definitely had the upper hand of the two emotions.

It should have been a wonderful moment (according to all those movies as well as many of his friends, at least) something that would stay within his memory for the rest of his life, a truly unforgettable time that he would treasure forever. And in truth, it *would* linger inside his head for the rest of his days – but for all the wrong reasons.

He had pleaded with his wife to be excused. *Begged* her to tell the midwife and doctor that she didn't want him present at the birth of their first child. Even though the poor woman had been suffering the agonies of labour for over six hours and had now been given an epidural to help numb the pain, he could only think of himself, of his phobia with blood, of his terror of hospitals and all things medical.

Then the unborn infant had shown signs of stress and the doctor roughly brushed the 'father' aside, telling him in no uncertain terms that he must remain in the room to comfort his wife while she carried out an emergency forceps delivery to save the baby's life.

As his wife endured the agonies of the cold metal forceps being pushed inside her, her husband could only squeeze her hand in a half-hearted attempt at easing her suffering and try to show his empathy with her plight, while in reality, he was battling with nausea and the overwhelming urge to pass out, right there on the delivery room floor.

Then, it was over. A nurse whipped the freshly born child over to some kind of device which sucked mucus and blood from the baby's nose, and it took its first gasping breath of air after nine months of living in fluid.

So, no smack on the backside from a hefty midwife, then? Another Hollywood myth blown out of the water.

The child was wrapped in a clean towel and handed unceremoniously to its mother. "It's a boy!" stated the midwife, enthusiastically, while the doctor worked feverishly with needle and suture to repair the damage to the mother's torn vagina, caused by the emergency use of the forceps.

Unremarkably, the mother began to throw up and the midwife pushed the tiny child into its father's arms before fetching a bowl for his wife.

Again, in the movies, the newborn babe is a lovely clean, pink colour with fluffy hair and rosy cheeks, whereas *this* baby was covered in a thick white creamy material, mingled with traces of his mother's blood.

It looks like snot … or spunk! the father couldn't help thinking as he gazed at his new son as though it were a creature from another world.

Then he looked at the misshapen head and involuntarily held the child at arm's length. Not only did the head look like the shape of a coconut, but it was also yellow! In fact, the boy's entire body was yellow. And worse yet, the baby was covered in thick, coarse, dark fur! The tiny arms, back and legs were as hairy as any chimp and hair grew like sideburns forming a tiny beard on the infant's trembling chin.

"Look mum, daddy's already bonding with his son!" cooed the midwife, mistakenly, as it happened. Nothing could be further from the truth in fact, as all 'daddy' wanted to do, was to hand the monkey-boy back to the midwife and get the hell out of there and have a stiff drink or ten.

But his wife was in a bad way; she had lost a lot of blood during the birth and she was in a state of collapse after the hours of labour. A worried looking doctor spoke in hushed tones to the midwife and much to the new father's relief, he was ushered out of the delivery room and instructed to remain in the waiting room until he was called for.

Okay, so it wasn't the stiff drink he really needed, but anything, *anything*, was better than being in that room with the kidney bowls of bloody instruments, and what could only be described as '*bits*' of his wife. That and umbilical cord and placenta and blood; lots of thick red blood.

*

She died that night without regaining consciousness. The doctor had missed the artery severed during the forceps procedure until it was far too late to do anything about it, and though they worked on his wife for a very long time, she was now a cold, dead body down in the mortuary.

And even *now*, all he could think about was himself! Never mind that she had suffered all that pain giving birth to their child; never mind that she was cold and lifeless and lying alone on a stainless steel tray deep in the bowels of the hospital. What would *he* do now? After all *he* was alone too, just him and ... oh God ... him and Monkey Boy, of course. The thought crossed his mind – more accurately, it didn't just cross, it remained resolutely within his brain, that he could flee the hospital, run away and leave Monkey Boy where he was in the nursery and never return, never see that misshapen skull, or yellow skin covered in thick, coarse hair again.

But then a very rare spasm of guilt entered his head. Even *he* couldn't leave the dead body of his wife in the hospital morgue. His mind conjured up the scenario of the police becoming involved if he didn't return and sort out 'the arrangements' for her burial. He could imagine the press getting hold of the story and dragging it out for weeks and months, his business would be ruined, his friends would desert him, his life would also be over just as surely as his wife's was. The newspaper headlines flashed before his self-pitying, tear-filled eyes;

Husband flees hospital after wife dies giving birth to Monkey Boy!

Cowardly 'father' leaves brave dead wife and horribly deformed baby to rot in hospital!

Those and a dozen other banner headlines ran through his mind, and he knew, for no other reason than self-preservation, he could not simply leave her there and slip out, unnoticed, into the night.

He also knew with a dawning horror that he couldn't leave his – the word almost refused to form in his head –his 'son', the Monkey Boy either.

*

As it turned out, the yellow tinge to the boy's skin was caused by a touch of jaundice, which was soon remedied. Also, the misshapen skull had apparently been caused by the forceps delivery and quickly returned to a more normally shaped skull after a few days. Even the 'thick fur' somehow rubbed off within a week or so "Perfectly natural – many babies have exactly the same thing at birth," he was told by a nurse, and she was right. The boy was now a healthy pink colour and had no more hair than any other baby of a similar age. "So, what are you going to call the little chap, then?" asked the nurse whose specialist subject appeared to be baby fur.

"I … er … I haven't thought about that just yet … a lot on my mind. You know how it is," he replied, lamely. The truth be told, he had only ever thought of the child as Monkey Boy since the birth, but at least he had the good sense not to tell anyone else of this. Even he realised that a child couldn't go through life with a name like Monkey Boy. Supposing he ended up going to Eton or Cambridge, what then?

"Well best to think of a name, and as soon as, just in case …" added the nurse, mysteriously. He had no idea what 'just in case' meant, but agreed to put some thought to the matter, more to shut her up than anything else.

He considered Kong and Cheetah briefly, but they were simply ludicrous notions. Damien was also in the running (after all, hadn't he killed *his* mother?) but that also was a tad obvious. Then, the idea to google the word 'death' came to him and that led him to Mors, mortis the Latin for death or 'of death' and he decided to corrupt these words into Morris which was what the child was finally called.

There would be no christening; his father figured that anyone who came into the world by causing the death of his own mother did not deserve the protection allegedly offered by such a sacred ritual. He would just have to fend for himself in that respect.

*

Morris was a strange baby from day one. He never cried, not ever; even when he was wet and hungry, he would just lie patiently in his cot until the rapidly hired nanny attended to his needs.

"He's such a wonderful baby!" she often enthused about her charge "Just a little angel, he is!" His father thought that 'angel' was just about the complete opposite of what the child really was. He would lie there, his big dark eyes staring up at his father, with no trace of emotion, no hint of a baby mind behind the steady, cold stare, just a chilling sensation that the adult was being studied by the baby like a specimen in a laboratory. His father was convinced that he had been brain damaged during the birth, but the hospital strenuously denied that anything of the sort had occurred. No, he was just a very quiet baby, perhaps unusually so, but by no means brain damaged.

Morris could speak fluently by the age of three. This in itself was not that strange, but there had been none of the usual baby language, no da da das, no goo goo goos, no blowing bubbles while learning to use his mouth for anything other than eating.

52

Boys Will be Boys

No, he simply couldn't speak and then he could; it was a simple as that, and none of the so-called experts could explain why. For once in Morris's short life, they couldn't use the well-worn phrase 'perfectly normal'.

He could also read. Not baby books, *real* books, proper novels, newspapers, scientific journals, in fact anything that he could lay his tiny, but unusually strong hands on, and no one had ever given the boy so much as a single second's worth of tuition in the fine art of learning to read.

He could also write, not childish nonsense, not fairy tales or silly rhymes, but proper adult prose together with a lot of technical stuff that even his father could barely understand.

Morris was thrown out of playgroup on the excuse that he wasn't 'engaging' either with the staff or the other children, but his father knew that he had intimidated the adults working there by studying them constantly and talking to them as though *they* were the children and he were the adult. He also refused point-blank to join in with any of the childish games or sing any of the infantile songs, and while the other children napped during 'quiet time', Morris would be found either engrossed in some mighty tome or would merely sit quietly staring at the staff as they nervously chatted amongst themselves, every so often casting a sideways glance in his direction.

Infant school was a similar experience of course; the headmistress confided to Morris's father that there was simply nothing they could possibly teach the boy. In fact, she admitted, the boy could undoubtedly teach some of her staff a thing or two!

So what to do with a five-year-old boy genius? Obviously far too young for secondary school, not mentally of course, but the boy would be tormented from day one by the older boys. And even though his father had no feelings towards the boy whatsoever, he didn't want his son to suffer needlessly.

Fortunately, aside from the fact that his father earned a very good living as the proprietor of a chain of successful estate

53

agencies, there had also been an insurance payout on the death of his wife as well as a hefty out of court settlement from the hospital in an attempt to keep their obvious negligence quiet. In short, they were a little more than comfortably off when it came to finances.

It was possible, therefore, to hire a private tutor for the boy, someone suitably qualified to teach such a young but incredibly intelligent child as Morris. It was possible, but very difficult as it turned out.

The first tutor, an elderly woman by the name of Doris Hoskins lasted only three days, before fleeing the house never to return. She babbled something about Morris being too strange to work with as she beat her hasty retreat, sending a friend round to collect her belongings a couple of days later.

The second tutor faired only slightly better by making it through the first week. He was a retired public school master who suddenly discovered the urgent need to visit a sick relative in Australia.

The third and fourth didn't see out a whole day between them, and the fifth simply refused to be interviewed for the job by a five-year-old child.

The sixth however, seemed to make everyone happy, Morris especially so. She was a woman in her late twenties by the name of Jayne Mitchell and had come very highly recommended by the agency employed to find the right sort of person for the job.

The boy's father was also smitten by the woman and they got on like the proverbial house on fire from the moment he opened the door and saw the very attractive, blue-eyed Jayne beaming a huge smile at him and offering him her delicately manicured hand to shake. Even Morris, who had never in his five years on earth been known to smile, had a fixed grin on his small face as he stared in open admiration at his new tutor.

At last, someone who both father and son liked and could get along with.

Within six weeks, the father and the new tutor were getting

along *very well* indeed and had started a passionate affair, with her creeping into his bedroom when Morris had gone to sleep and staying there all night, every night.

Morris was very quick to notice the changes in Jayne and his father. He noticed the way that they looked at each other, he spotted the way they brushed against one another when passing in the hall or kitchen, he spied his father playfully pinch her perfectly shaped bottom and saw the way she giggled when he did so.

He noticed all these things and for the very first time in his life, Morris was feeling confused. Confused and another emotion, which, after researching through several books he discovered was called jealousy.

Being an emotionless child throughout his life, Morris wasn't sure that jealousy was the correct diagnosis for this new felt emotion, but something was definitely wrong with him. And, if this was indeed jealousy, of what or whom was he jealous, exactly? This was something he couldn't understand, something which although he could look it up in a reference book and understand the words he read within, he couldn't apply the learnt facts to himself, he couldn't figure out the root cause of this feeling, and it bothered Morris – it bothered him a lot.

Six months had now passed and the boy, though still deeply puzzled by these strange sensations, was still happy in his own way with life and with his tutor in particular. He had never known any real love or affection, but he was sure that Jayne loved him. She was always very kind towards him at least and used to playfully ruffle his hair when he managed to solve a particularly difficult question, which he of course invariably did. He found the hair ruffling very annoying at first, until he realised that this was her way of showing him affection, or love.

So when Morris was called into the study that evening, the sight of Jayne and his father holding hands on the settee, both with huge grins on their faces, left him open-mouthed in amazement..

"Ah … Morris …" his father began, nervously, "Jayne and I … well … we've decided to um … get married. Jayne will become your mother." And as if to confirm the fact, Jayne held up her left hand to show Morris the large diamond engagement ring which glinted brilliantly on her finger and she flashed the boy an equally brilliant, wide smile of happiness.

Morris's reaction took the happy couple completely by surprise. Initially, he stood with a puzzled frown creasing his young brow, but moments later, he rushed across the room and threw both arms around Jayne's, neck hugging her close.

"Oh mummy, I love you!" and there were, incredibly, tears in the five-year-old's eyes. Morris had never been known to shed so much as a single tear in his entire life, so this was a complete revelation for his stunned father. The boy clung to Jayne's neck for an uncomfortably long time, and she was forced to ease him gently away from her so that she could breathe.

"Don't you think you ought to congratulate daddy as well, Morris?" she asked quietly.

Morris stepped back and wiped the tears from his eyes with the back of his hand. He took a long look at Jayne and then at his father. Then, he shook his father's hand as you would shake a stranger's.

"Congratulations, Father," was all the boy said, almost, but not quite, grudgingly. There had never been any sort of affection between father and son, and it seemed to be an ordeal for them both.

"Thank you, Morris. I'm pleased that you're happy with the news."

Morris turned his attention back to Jayne and smiled.

"I'm *very* happy, thank you. And now, if you'll please excuse me?" And with that he left the study, closing the door quietly behind him.

"Strange boy, that one," said his father upon hearing his son running upstairs to his bedroom. "Very strange."

Jayne leant across and kissed her future husband full on the lips.

"He's just a kid. A very *intelligent* kid, but a kid all the same, and now he's a *happy* kid at that. We have no idea what it must be like to lose a mother at your birth – it's enough to make *anyone* a little odd, knowing that they died bringing you into the world."

Her fiancé pulled her close to him and gently kissed her forehead.

"I guess you're right, Jayne. I've never really thought of it like that," he said, but he was also thinking: But why the hell was he so weird even as a baby? He had no idea about his mother dying in childbirth back then; but he kept the thought to himself.

Morris lay on his bed, arms crossed behind his head, legs crossed at the ankles, eyes wide and staring up at the ceiling. He was experiencing another strange emotion, or was it the same one he'd felt the other day only in a different form? He was perplexed about the whole thing and had no idea what to think. As always, he decided that further information was required to enable him to make a balanced judgement on the matter.

He had read and outgrown every reference book in the house and Jayne had talked his father into buying the five-year-old boy a laptop which would open up the whole world of knowledge to the child. Morris sat up on his bed, flipped open the laptop and switched it on.

He typed the word EMOTIONS into the search engine and waited for the results.

Morris was busy reading very late into the night, way past his usual nine-thirty bedtime and he was perturbed by both the articles he read and perhaps more so by the strange noises coming from the direction of his father's bedroom. Noises which could be construed either as pleasure or of pain, he could not decide which, noises culminating in Jayne screaming "Yes! Yes! Yes!" before the sounds ended and the house fell silent once more.

Silent that is, apart from the gentle tapping of Morris's small fingers on his laptop keypad as he now decided that further investigation was needed on the matter of these strange sounds coming from his father's room.

*

The boy was late getting up the next morning, which in itself was unusual, as Morris was *never* late in rising. Jayne took one look at his pale, tired face and asked, "Are you okay, Morris, you look very white this morning?" and she placed a cool hand against his forehead to see if the boy had developed a temperature in the night.

Jayne's hand against his brow felt somehow very pleasant, and an involuntary shudder made its way through the boy's body.

"Morris, you're shaking! You are definitely not well, young man, so back to bed for you I think!" she said, and took him by his clammy little hand and led him over to the staircase.

"I'm alright, thank you, just a little tired this morning. I didn't sleep very well last night," replied the boy, gripping tightly onto Jayne's hand as he spoke.

The thought crossed her mind that maybe he had heard their passionate love making of the previous evening, and Jayne blushed automatically. She smiled nervously at the boy and said "I hope nothing disturbed you, kept you awake?"

Morris looked her squarely in the eye and held her gaze. "No, nothing disturbed me. Why would it?"

Jayne tried to disguise the relief in her expression, but it was impossible with Morris's eyes boring into hers. Attack was her only defence.

"Well, whatever kept you awake, young man, it's back to bed for you for a few hours to catch up on your sleep!" and she playfully patted his scrawny rump and pointed a well-manicured finger towards his room.

The boy did as he was told, as he always did in fact, and returned to his room. He climbed under the covers but couldn't sleep. The only thing in his young mind were the images he had seen on various websites last night. Images of men and women coupled together in various positions, with the women calling out as Jayne had called out to his father last night. "YES! YES! YES," they screamed and said other things like "FUCK ME! FUCK ME!" and although they seemed to be in pain during those acts, they also appeared to be enjoying it as well. Once again, Morris was feeling confused by the whole gamut of emotions now affecting, or perhaps *infecting* his mind.

But one thing seemed absolutely clear to him; these were definitely the same sounds that he had heard the previous evening, sounds made by his father and Jayne as they did the same things he had witnessed other couples doing on the websites he had visited.

Things that he realised could only lead to one ultimate result if they were to continue. And that thought brought yet another new emotion crashing into his five-year-old mind.

*

The wedding arrangements seemed to be all that Jayne and his father could talk about so far as Morris was concerned. It had originally been planned to take place in mid-August, hopefully during a beautiful summer's day, but for reasons unknown to the boy, the wedding had been hurriedly brought forward and would now take place in just over four weeks time, coincidentally, the happy event would occur only two days after Morris's sixth birthday.

"We can have a *double* celebration, Morris!" enthused Jayne as she ruffled the boy's hair in her usual manner. Morris smiled dutifully, but mused that none of his previous birthdays had ever been a cause for celebration, so why would this one be any different?

Then the bombshell was dropped; the very scenario that Morris had both envisaged and dreaded beyond anything else in life, came to pass.

Jayne and his father were sitting as before on the sofa in the study. They linked hands as though their very lives depended on the close contact as father asked Morris to take a seat.

"Er … Morris …" began his father. "I have some wonderful news to tell you …" Father looked particularly nervous while Jayne beamed a huge smile at her future husband and squeezed his hand as though to urge him on with telling of the 'wonderful news'.

He cleared his throat and continued.

"We … Jayne and I … are … we're …" his voice petered out. He knew the words, had rehearsed them several times before calling the boy into the study, but simply could not say them.

Jayne smiled, squeezed his hand once more and continued on his behalf.

"What your father is *trying* to tell you, is that you are going to have a baby brother or sister, Morris! Great news, isn't it!?" and as Jayne and his father stared in goggle-eyed admiration and love for one another, they failed to notice the look of horror on Morris's five-year-old face.

The boy turned on his heel and left the room, closing the door quietly behind him. "MORRIS!" his father bellowed, angry that the moment, their *special* moment, hadn't met with at least some sign of enthusiasm, a token 'congratulations', anything but silence and departure.

He made to stand up and follow the boy, but Jayne pulled him back.

"Leave him, darling, he's in shock at the news, that's all. It's only been you and him for so long, and now suddenly, there'll be *four* people sharing this house. It's a lot to take in, and after all, he *is* only five years old, no matter how smart he may be, he's just a very young kid at heart." Jayne leaned across and kissed the father of her unborn child passionately on the lips.

60

Boys Will be Boys

"He'll come round, you'll see," she added, afterwards.

*

Morris was lying on his bed, arms folded behind his head in his usual thinking mode. But *unusually*, there were tears in his eyes; tears of anger and of self-pity and of bewilderment. All of the confused and unwelcome emotions he had been experiencing since Jayne had arrived in the house, had finally bubbled over in one huge cascade of jumbled feelings which had erupted into stinging tears and choking sobs.

Morris had actually begun to believe that things were improving in his life. He had someone, Jayne, who actually seemed to care about him, his father had shown him an almost considerate side never before witnessed, since her arrival and the whole house seemed a better place in which to live, his life had been changing for the better.

But now this. It had been inevitable, he realised that much, but so soon? Just when, for the first time in his life he was getting some attention, some affection, it would have to be shared with another. And Morris was wise enough to know that his share of the love would be considerably outweighed by the portion which would be heaped upon the new baby – *their* baby, a shared part of *them* created when they made those noises every night in father's bedroom along the landing.

Morris sat upright on his bed and wiped the tears from his eyes with the cuff of his jumper. He rubbed a hand across his face as though wiping sleep from his eyes. No more tears, he told himself. There would be no more crying and no more emotions from him. He had let things get to him, and this was the result.

The boy left the bed and walked to his desk where he flipped on his laptop and waited for it to come to life. It was almost dawn before he finally switched it off and climbed into his bed, falling asleep within moments.

Boys Will be Boys

*

It was Morris's sixth birthday and Jayne and his father had managed to find the time in between making the last minute arrangements for their big day as well as visits to the hospital for prenatal check ups and scans, to organise a small party for him.

'Small' being the operative word, as Morris had no friends and no opportunity to make any. Anyway, he would have had as much in common with an average six-year-old as he would have had with a dinosaur. And at least he would have found the dinosaur a lot more interesting.

So, the 'party' consisted of his father and Jayne, his former nanny and, as his father had no living parents or siblings, a distant aunt and her equally distant daughter.

Morris was both embarrassed at being the centre of attention and annoyed at the way his former nanny and this great aunt whom he had never heard of before, made such a fuss over him.

"He was a *wonderful* lickle baby," crowed the nanny. "A proper *angel*, he was. Never cried, did you, poppet?" And she pinched his cheek, affectionately as Morris squirmed and tried to escape back to the safety of his room, only then to be cornered by the great aunt and her dopey looking daughter.

"You look so much like your mother, Morris. The dead spit of her, you are!" she said, before turning to her daughter. "You remember Aunty Jill, don't you, Celia; doesn't Morris look like her, eh?" But Celia looked as though she may well struggle to recall her *own* image, even if she had had a mirror in front of her to help.

No one had ever mentioned the fact that he looked like his late mother before then. He considered that maybe *this* was the reason that his father had despised him so much over the years. But then again, until Jayne entered the house that day, his father seemed to have despised just about everyone, so maybe that had nothing to do with it, after all.

Finally, after what seemed like a lifetime, the party was over and the guests, such as they were, had left. There were a few childish toys and games given to Morris as presents left unopened and unplayed-with on the floor beside the settee. Jayne and his father were clearing away plates and glasses, feeding them into the dishwasher and busily chatting about the wedding in two days time, when Morris interrupted them in the kitchen.

"Thank you for my party – it was nice," he offered, half-heartedly.

"That's okay, Morris, glad you enjoyed yourself," replied Jayne. "Now it's off to bed for you, young man; you've had a busy day," she added.

Morris could hear them talking about the wedding once more as he climbed the stairs to his room, his birthday already forgotten as they engrossed themselves in their plans for the future, and the future of the new baby.

*

The gentle, muffled tapping sound woke Jayne first. The curtains were drawn, but she could see daylight creeping around the edges and she glanced across at the bedside clock. Eight twenty-five a.m.

Then there was another light knock on the door. Jayne pulled the duvet around her to cover her nakedness and called out, "Yes, come in?" as Morris's father stirred beside her.

The door opened slowly, and in came Morris carrying a tray heaped with breakfast things, making his way carefully across the gloomily lit room and setting it down gently on Jayne's bedside table.

"There!" he said, "you made me a birthday party and I've made you breakfast in bed!" And he smiled broadly, before opening the curtains and flooding the bedroom with early morning light.

His father struggled to sit up, his eyes squinting against the

63

sudden brightness, and said "Whatsup? What's going on?"

"Nothing's up, darling. Morris has kindly brought us breakfast as a reward for giving him a party yesterday," replied Jayne.

"Ah … right … thank you, Morris … very kind I'm sure."

Morris smiled tightly and said, "I'll leave you to it then. There's tea, coffee, orange juice, toast and marmalade. Enjoy!" And he left the room, closing the bedroom door behind him, before putting his ear to the thin wooden panelling to listen, hearing his father express his incredulity while Jayne laughed quietly as he spluttered his amazement.

*

Morris left them for one and a half hours before he returned to their bedroom.

He had calculated that would be more than enough time for the drugs mixed in the tea, coffee and orange juice to take effect. He had already experimented on a neighbour's cat and had simply extrapolated his results to account for the increased body mass of adult humans.

Thank God for the Internet, he thought. You could buy, almost, anything on there these days; his father's credit card had also helped of course. He had tried, however, to buy Rohypnol, but discovered that it was banned in many countries, and anyway, his research had led him to believe that it wouldn't be powerful enough for his needs.

So, he had looked further and had discovered that Ketamin mixed with a small amount of chloral hydrate should be ideal, and his experiments with the cat confirmed this. Alas, his first trials with a couple of squirrels in the large back garden of the detached house had gone badly wrong, leaving one stone dead and the other permanently paralysed down one half of its body.

*

He opened the bedroom door cautiously and peered inside. They were both still there and completely motionless. Jayne was out for the count and lying on her side, but his father was lying propped up on his pillows with his eyes wide open, staring straight ahead.

Morris checked on Jayne first. He felt her pulse. It was slow but steady.

Then he checked his father. He was quite shocked to see his father's eyes trying to track him across the room as Morris made his way around the king-sized bed towards him, but Morris realised that this ability to see what was going on, what was about to happen, would make the whole thing more enjoyable and worthwhile.

The boy left the room and soon returned with another breakfast tray, only this one was covered with a tea towel from the kitchen. Morris set the tray down carefully on his father's bedside table and whipped the tea towel away before tilting his father's paralysed head so that he could see the array of knives and other implements arranged carefully upon it.

A look of sheer terror came into his eyes and Morris noted with delight, that his father was trying to call out, to move, to run away. But he remained motionless. The combination of drugs was working well and would continue to do so for some time to come. Time enough for Morris to complete his work at least.

Morris stripped off the duvet and threw it into a corner of the room. He noticed that both of the adults were naked, which was good as it saved him the trouble of struggling to remove any nightclothes.

He then flipped Jayne over onto her back and arranged her ready to carry out the operation he had watched several times on the Internet. He had paid very careful attention to detail and had made scrupulous notes to aid him.

Morris selected a couple of very sharp kitchen knives from the tray beside his father, and as an afterthought, he picked up a pair of garden secateurs as well and popped them into his back pocket. He had decided only last night, that he would operate on Jayne first, so that his helpless father could have the pleasure of watching the whole thing, knowing that *he* was to blame for the situation.

With this in mind, Morris adjusted his father's head so that he could better see what was about to happen.

Morris opened Jayne's legs and spread them wide. Most six-year-olds had never seen a vagina before, but Morris had been doing his homework and had seen plenty, one way or another, on the Internet and was completely unfazed by the experience.

He took a small knife and jabbed it into her genitalia, just to ensure that Jayne was out for the count. When there was no reaction, he plunged the knife deep into her lower abdomen and started to cut across just above the pubic bone as he had seen surgeons doing as they performed Caesarean section deliveries.

The knife was sharp, but no scalpel, and it took Morris quite some time to hack his way across so that the opening was large enough for him to see what he was doing for the next phase of the procedure.

The sheets and mattress were now covered in blood and Morris had to keep wiping his small hands on a towel taken from their en suite bathroom as the knife was becoming too slippery.

After several minutes of delving about inside Jayne, Morris was certain that he had found what he was looking for and removed it with a few cuts of the kitchen knife.

Satisfied, he withdrew the uterus and dropped it, unceremoniously on the bed between Jayne and his father. He briefly considered sewing up the gaping slash, but then quickly discounted the idea as a waste of time. And what would be the point anyway? She was going nowhere.

Morris turned his attention to the uterus, and quickly located the small sack containing the tiny foetus, his would-have-been brother or sister. The foetus was just as he had seen in books and on the Internet. It looked more alien than human at this stage of its existence with the head disproportionately larger than its body, and, making certain that his father could see clearly, he had no compunction in snipping of his sibling's head with the secateurs.

Morris allowed himself another rare smile. It was a job well done, a successful operation.

Now it was father's turn, and a much simpler procedure.

Once again, Morris adjusted the paralysed man's head so that he could clearly see what was about to happen, this time, to him. Only his father's eyes gave any hint that he was aware of the horror of it all, but he was completely unable to prevent it from happening or even close his eyelids to block it from his vision.

Morris held his father's penis in his left hand and stretched it so that the testicles were dangling like two fat plums. Then, he picked up the secateurs once more and snipped through his father's manhood at the very base, holding his trophy triumphantly before the adult's eyes, blood dripping from the severed scrotum and forming a gory puddle on his chest.

"There!" said the boy, "That'll stop you two having anymore children, I think!" Morris left the room while his father was forced to remain staring at his butchered crotch, the blood welling up from between his thighs in thick, red gouts.

Morris struggled back into the room with the heavy cans of petrol and placed them just inside the bedroom door. He then gathered up all his equipment and took them down to the kitchen before returning to gather up the drugged breakfast things. He carefully cleaned every item in boiling water laced with bleach, making sure that there was no trace of blood and just as importantly, no remaining sign of the drugs he had used. He had already dumped the bottles they had arrived in into a bottle bank, several miles from his home.

Satisfied that every trace had been removed, he closed the kitchen door and headed up to his 'parents' bedroom.

His father was by now trying to move. Morris could see the fingers of his left hand twitching and a faint movement in his left foot. Good, the boy thought. He would not only know what was happening, but would also feel everything as well.

Morris unscrewed the tops from the petrol cans and began pouring it around the room, paying particular attention to the two people on the bed and ensuring that they were thoroughly dowsed in the highly flammable liquid.

He removed the petrol cans from the bedroom, took a new box of Swan Vestas from his pocket, showing them to his terrified father, before stepping back to the doorway, lighting a couple of matches and flicking them onto the bed.

Despite his research, he was quite shocked at the powerful way the fire ignited and took hold of the room. Within seconds, it was ablaze and Morris only just had time to shut the door before the flames reached him.

He hurried downstairs and returned the cans to the large triple garage where he had found them. The garage directly beneath his father's bedroom. The garage where, when Morris calculated enough time had elapsed to destroy completely all evidence of what he had done to the two adults now being cremated within, he would set another fire, which he was confident, would disguise the one he had lit in the room above.

When the floor gave way, and the upstairs bedroom crashed into the garage below, even the best fire investigation officer would be unable to tell where it had initially started.

*

And after all, Morris was just a six-year-old kid. Kids played with matches, didn't they? He'd be very sorry, he'd clearly been very naughty, but then, boys will be boys, won't they?

BEHIND THE SCREEN

Gary Fry

"Come on, just one quick look," Jake said, keeping his eyes firmly fixed on his laptop's screen.

The one thing he missed while away alone on fieldwork was physical intimacy. The wonders of the Internet had provided an adequate alternative, however: the messenger program, which allowed him to speak to his wife while watching her at the same time. At thirty-six, Zoe was still worth looking at, and if Jake was less interested these days in what she had to say – it was usually tiresome, repetitive stuff about the kids – he could at least console himself by thinking that, unlike the wives of many of his colleagues at the department, she was still interested in modestly deviant sexual fun and games.

"Just slip the top down, show me your nipples," he said as Zoe gave him a slightly intolerant glance. The digital screen, with its low frame-rate, rendered this expression piecemeal and jerky, yet perceptible all the same. Nevertheless, Jake adjusted the zip at the front of his trousers, as if in anticipation of imminent pleasure. "I just need something to help me come off, you know. I'm … I'm lonely here."

"Oh, you mean, there's *not* a bar downstairs, Jake? Don't forget I saw the photos of the hotel on the Internet. It looked like a swanky joint."

"Yeah, but it's also in the middle of nowhere, next to a bloody field outside of Ipswich. And it's early February – hardly a busy period. In fact, the place is pretty much empty. Just a couple of saddos trying to chat the barmaid up. And believe me, they've *no* chance."

"Tried and failed, have you?"

"Why else would I be trying to get my excitement from you on a tiny bit of LCD?"

"LCD? Now you sound like you're on drugs," said Zoe, but then clearly adjusted the laptop she had in front of her (this

69

was one of four in the household; for a mere government-employed researcher, Jake's wage was pretty healthy), tugged up the folds of her sweater, lifted the material and finally revealed her breasts, large and round, with only the slightest trace of sagging.

Jake took out his penis at once.

"Keep them visible, darling. That's the way," he said, and started to masturbate. Strangely, despite his and his wife's long-term sexual openness, he'd always preferred not to let Zoe see his hand at work during this familiar procedure. A few minutes later he ejaculated onto a pre-prepared tissue laid out on the single bed in this single room, two hundred miles south of his home in Leeds. Once he'd managed to subsume the pulsing throes of what now suddenly felt like a furtive act, he checked the clock in the bottom-right corner of his laptop's screen. It was only nine p.m. He could go down to the bar, after all, and maybe have a few beers.

After Zoe was fully clothed again, and they'd exchanged fond farewells (in truth, his were rather less fond than the warmness he'd expressed after dialling into the online conversation ten minutes earlier) Jake disengaged his webcam, leaving only a grainy image of his wife seated in their lounge. She'd clearly placed her own machine on one arm of the couch, the better to free her body for all that necessary movement. But then the whole of her winked out with a hiss of technological static, and Jake was finally free.

He loved Zoe, but he had to admit that these half-week fieldwork trips were always hugely welcome. After interviewing clients in a variety of deprived social conditions, he could make use of the department's expenses account and visit the kind of restaurants he couldn't really afford to take the whole family to. He missed the kids, too, though only in principle; in truth, a few days without their constant eight- and ten-year-old bickering was something quite close to bliss. Frankly, he didn't know how his wife coped with being just a housewife. Yes, working life certainly had its stresses, but at least it also offered a little freedom.

Once he'd exited his room, paced downstairs in the largely deserted hotel, and entered the bar, Jake saw another couple of guys much like himself, slumped over pints and reading newspapers: a pink, important broadsheet for bald head in the corner; a cheap and cheerful tabloid for the laddish-looking guy huddled beside the fruit machine. There was in fact a *third* man in this small bar area, though Jake hadn't immediately noticed him. He seemed to have emerged from a trick of light and perspective, seated on a tall stool at the bar itself and nursing a short measure of something bronze which glistened. Beyond him, the barmaid – a pretty young thing with a nametag pinned to one eye-thrilling breast – didn't appear to be taking much interest in her guests, and Jake's arrival looked unlikely to lead to any immediate change in this attitude.

Still, when he reached the bar, the woman stepped forwards from behind it, her high heels making an echoic sound like special audio effects on some tinny computer. *Christ*, thought Jake immediately, shaking his tired old head. *I've been working far too hard, typing up my notes, scouring the Internet, Lord knows what else …*

"Can I help you?" the barmaid said, her tone professionally courteous yet lacking any soul or conviction. Perhaps she was single and really hated her job. It couldn't be much fun being female *and* having to earn a living; Jake sometimes wondered whether his wife knew how lucky she was.

"A scotch, please. Threaten it with ice, though don't make it too submissive."

"You what?"

"He wants the same as me."

This latest comment had been spoken by the guy seated on the bar stool – the one Jake hadn't really spotted upon entering a minute ago. Now he had a chance to take a proper look at him, he noticed he was just as innocuous in appearance as might have been imagined. He wore a grey suit, sported a grey moustache, and was slightly balding with grey hair around his

71

ears. He was, frankly, the greyest man Jake had ever seen. Even his flesh had a bland, lifeless hue about it. And his smile when it came was as thin and unconvincing as the kind of night attire Jake had been trying to get his wife to wear during twelve years of marriage (and had succeeded on only two occasions: once on his thirtieth birthday, and the other after he'd given her five hundred pounds to go shopping in London – and God bless Ladbrokes for that one).

Jake glanced back at the barmaid and said, "Like the man says: same as him." Then, since the situation seemed to demand such an offer and Jake couldn't find a respectable way of pulling free from this tacit and frustrating obligation, he sat on the next available stool before adding, "And put another in his glass, too. I'm sure he'll reciprocate when the moment is right."

The barmaid appeared not to have even acknowledged the grey man's presence, though a moment later she cut away, took two chunky glasses from a shelf above the bar, turned around and started to unleash premeasured quantities from the most regal looking optic in the row. Chunks of ice followed with a sound like an old man's bones breaking. And then the drinks were on the bar top, Jake was feeling for his wallet, the filthy transaction was completed, and the barmaid had performed her existential flit anew: she simply stood there in one corner, pretending the universe wasn't happening, with a sullen, know-nothing-about-life expression on her face.

"What game are you in, my friend?" Jake asked the man beside him, once the first of the fiery liquid had started feeling for his guts with its hot and piercing fingers.

"Insurance," replied the guy, and then responded to Jake's opening slurp of scotch with ill-timed grace. Wasn't the unspoken rule, now Jake reflected on the matter, to take one's first drink with a companion *simultaneously*, the better to establish a complicit bond? But the man had waited at least ten seconds before setting about his own fresh supply.

And *insurance*, he'd said – was that going to be Jake's only answer? This certainly appeared to be the case; the man didn't look likely to add more. But Jake had never been so reticent about his own working life; in fact, he volunteered equivalent information without even being asked.

"I'm in social research," he explained, thinking it unlikely that, here in the bar, anybody other than Mr Grey would be able to hear him. The music on the jukebox was playing softly and yet insistently – something melodramatic about true love and contentment. "Yeah, I'm currently conducting a project about folk who lack sufficient funds to really get on in life, to affect their futures and steer their destinies. You know what I'm saying?"

"Mentally ill people?" the man asked immediately, and as he did so his face seemed to lose a little definition in the soft light of the room. Shadows undeniably clustered around each side of his head, as if the front of it was about to become detached. There was a strange and vacant look in his grey, watching eyes. For some reason, Jake was suddenly forced to think of maggots … But he now had the guy's question to answer.

"The mentally ill? Well, yes, it could be them. Or migrants newly arrived in the country. Or substance abusers." Jake took another pull from his whisky glass: the fierce stuff was now performing more of its usual magic inside him, and yet curiously, with the man's weirdly staring eyes still boring into him, Jake felt slightly uppity – nervous, even. Still, he managed to get through this brief uncertain period the only way he knew how: by babbling incessantly.

About five minutes later, the grey guy knew as much about Jake as Jake thought he might know about himself. He didn't regard himself as a complex man; rather, he considered himself honest, flawed, humble, and even a modest hypocrite. He was fully aware of the very obvious friction between interviewing underprivileged people and his mild exploitation of the department's expenses system. He also recalled that he'd quickly tried to dismiss his wife after she'd helped bring him to orgasm earlier. He was no fool, and he understood that the persona he chose to present to the world was merely an amiable mask, designed to coax and coerce. However, with regard to any of these shortcomings, could he actually stop himself? Well, the simple answer to that was that he had no desire to, not at all.

As Jake was in the last throes of his monologue, the grey man asked from deep within that pale disc of a face, "Where do you live?"

Jake told him. By now they were into their second servings of scotch (the barmaid had again come and gone with remarkable indifference). Jake even gave the man his postcode. And then he finished with giddy, slightly slurred words: "Don't get me wrong, mate. I love my wife and kids, but sometimes I just wish … well, it's *only* sometimes, but it's *sometimes* all the same … yes, sometimes I *wish I'd remained a single man.* You know what I'm saying here?"

"I know it well, for I am he," replied the grey man, and this time those insectile eyes – their dark pupils twitching like ants drenched in some kind of glutinous ointment – grew wide and cold and needy.

Jake felt suddenly uncomfortable, but he somehow managed to reply, "What, you mean, you *don't* have any kids? Or a … a *fucking wife?*" By now the whisky was feeling for him with long and tactile limbs, pulling him under its indomitable command. "Fuck me, you lucky bastard." He laughed, snarled with the booze, and then added, "Oh, you lucky, lucky bastard."

At that moment Jake noticed in his peripheral vision that the other two guys in the bar – bald-head and babe-magnet – were standing to leave. Maybe it was simply getting late. Surely their departure wasn't in response to anything he'd just said. As they passed, they each fiddled with their mobile phones, as if they were expecting contact at any moment on these devices. Rings of silver twinkled amid their splayed left hands. Then they were gone, leaving only Jake, the grey guy and the barmaid (who obviously had no choice but to remain).

However, a moment later the man – or insect-eyes, as Jake had, at some restless subconscious level, begun to think of him – shifted from his stool, glanced at Jake, and said, "Thanks for the drink. And thanks for downloading everything inside you into me." And then he was also gone, marching swiftly and silently for the doorway that led up to all the hotel's sporadically occupied rooms this evening, in this chill season, and in this relatively unpopular part of the country.

Something about the grey guy's parting words lingered in Jake's mind, and he soon found himself turning his attentions to the barmaid. He pointed to his now empty glass. "Another in here, sweetheart," he instructed, the way his father had always asked for stuff from young women in menial roles when Jake had been just a child. His mother hadn't ever appeared to mind, and it was only later – several years later – that the old man had left her for a younger woman, leaving Jake with little choice but to support his mother, as well as a wife and two growing kids.

When the fresh drink was at last clicked down in front of him, Jake started to soliloquise. "Man, life's a bitch and then you marry … Oh, sorry, what was that? Three-twenty, is it? Same as last time, hee hee. Here's a fiver. You keep the change, my love. Buy yourself something nice to wear for your boyfriend. You … you *do* have a boyfriend, don't you?"

It must have been a good hour later that he finally climbed into bed, having made no progress with the spectacularly aloof barmaid. He slept with a thunderous disposition, his dreams portentous and laden with images which any shrink worth his salt would consider ripe for rich interpretive analysis. When he awoke the following morning, however, all he could recall from these nocturnal imaginings were two creeping-crawling eyes locked in a flimsy face . . .

At work that day he interviewed a family of travellers who'd lacked any formal schooling and were trying to get by in life by selling handmade goods from one place to another. After he'd acquired this data, Jake went to a pub in nearby

Colchester and ordered a cheapish meal of pie and chips. He'd now been away from home for three whole days; he'd noticed in the past that by this stage he'd start to miss a few domestic comforts and not just the obvious ones. Frankly, he reflected as he got in his car and headed back for his hotel, he could use a cuddle right now. But he knew his wife's face and voice on the Internet messenger program would serve almost as well.

After he'd parked in the forecourt of the building, he climbed out under the dimming late-winter sky. It was about four o'clock. The kids were usually home from school on the bus at half-past. With any luck, Jake would catch Zoe alone. He locked up his vehicle, stepped across for the hotel entrance, ignored the fat middle-aged woman smiling broadly behind the reception desk and went immediately upstairs.

Once he'd reached his room, he hung the DO NOT DISTURB sign on the external door handle, and then, after flinging himself onto the bed, switched on his laptop. In the late afternoon, his wife ordinarily went online to catch up with her favourite TV shows, so Jake could be reasonably sure Zoe would be available if he dropped her a quick email now. He did precisely that, waited a short while for the message to be acknowledged, and then, a few minutes later, a link was established between here and his gaff up north.

Jake looked at his screen.

And felt terror instantly drop a beaker of ice-cold water down his entire body.

The image in the small degraded window was certainly that of his lounge, but the figure seated at its centre wasn't his wife. Zoe's laptop was again clearly perched on one arm of the couch, and this person – it was a man, a *man* – was slumped against its other. He remained as still as death and was staring directly forwards, away from the onlooking webcam.

It was the grey man Jake had met last night in the hotel's bar downstairs.

Even though a dreadful species of fear continued to work at his bowels with adroit and deceptive fingertips, Jake could do nothing other than watch as the man started slowly turning his head the way of the camera – the way of Jake. Defying his natural instinct to turn away, Jake noticed that although their lower halves were out of shot, the man's legs were slightly elevated, as if his feet were rested on something. But Jake knew well there was nothing resembling a pouffe or a footstool in his lounge. He could recall his wife mentioning quite recently that she might like to acquire something of this description, perhaps once Jake had made her allowance available either this month or the next, but he was pretty sure she hadn't got around to buying one yet. There was, after all, the kids and their everyday financial needs to prioritise.

So what *were* the guy's elevated feet resting upon?

At that moment Jake pictured his wife, butchered and prostrate on the lounge's carpet. He also wondered, with beguiling transfixion, how on earth the man had got hold of his address. Had he raided Jake's room last night while Jake had been downstairs in the bar, half-heartedly trying to chat up that barmaid (oh, but he *wouldn't* have pursued this any further, even if she had proved receptive to his wiles)? Had the grey guy then driven maniacally north, with every intention of invading Jake's home? And had envy been his motivation? Yes, through a haze of all that swiftly imbibed alcohol, Jake could recall the man admitting that he had no family of his own, just before Jake had told him that … that …

Jake's mind was suddenly all a-fluster. His heart rate soared and then levelled out at an absurdly rapid speed, rendering his chest tight and painful.

And then the man on the screen, his digital image grainy and dreamlike, did what he simply had to do next.

He began to remove his face.

The pale disc of skin, little more than a lifelike mask, came quickly free with deftly applied fingertips. Shadows immediately accumulated on each side of his head, and a moment later the front section was completely free. The man detached it, before resting this flopping patch of flesh aside on one of the couch's cushions. And then, having turned momentarily away to tackle this impromptu amputation, he was glancing back into Zoe's webcam.

The dark area where the man's face had been only seconds earlier was now a crude oval of writhing insects: maggots, flies, ants, spiders, and more, more, more. All these creatures crawled back and forth across the sinewy ruin that was the guy's bleeding skull. Angular legs waded in blood; pale fluttery wings were caked in gore. And from within this insectile carnival, two grey eyes stared hard at Jake.

Jake jerked back, feeling sick after the cheap meal he'd eaten earlier. He suddenly pictured the gypsy family in their caravan, as well as so many more of the deprived people he'd interviewed recently. Then his attention switched back to the grey man, who, despite an absence of lips, was now smiling his bony, silk-thin smile.

From elsewhere in the property trapped alive, like something caught in amber, inside the computer ahead of Jake, a door was opened and shut. And then, seconds later, juvenile shouts and squabbling struck up, shattering the previous silence in the house.

For one awful moment, Jake was grateful that he wasn't at home to deal with his raucous family – this was an old habit of thought, mentally ingrained – but then he realised what was happening there.

His kids – Jessie and Duane, eight and ten years old – had just arrived back from school.

And the faceless figure, with that unnaturally writhing expression and its feet still strangely elevated in Jake's lounge, was now prepared to offer them a monstrous welcome.

THE OTHER TENANT

Mark Samuels

Robert Zachary first became aware of the tenant in the next-door apartment a week after moving in. He never saw the person on the landing that connected their two flats, and did not hear anything that indicated his or her comings and goings. Rather it was the sound of the television set filtering through the thin wall after midnight and continuing until dawn that provided confirmation of occupancy.

Zachary's neighbour appeared to be a devotee of strange and disturbing pre-recorded programmes, because the noise, though crackling and static-riddled, incorporated screams, moans, and long monologues of a macabre, even deranged, nature.

Doubtless these programmes constituted the other tenant's own personal selection, because Zachary could not track the broadcasts on any of the channels currently being transmitted, even with recourse to an up-to-date and extensive terrestrial, cable and satellite guide.

Perhaps, he thought, the other tenant only had access to a series of video cassettes of debased quality, for the ruinous sound quality did not indicate the high-end reproduction afforded by modern digital formats, and the acute analogue interference even ruled out a rogue satellite channel specifically tuned into from outside the range of those that are generally available.

Had Zachary slept in accordance with the usual workaday pattern, the one he had followed for the last thirty years, and had his sleeping routine not been severely disrupted by months of illness he might not have developed the obsessive fascination with the viewing habits of the tenant next door. But the lack of an organised daily routine, such as he'd long become accustomed to when employed by the television news company as a journalist, had meant that the hours he was awake and the hours he slept were a confused maze of time.

There were times when he discovered it was impossible to sleep before five a.m., some where he was exhausted by midday, and others where he had slept through an entire twenty-four hour period altogether.

Being only a few years shy of retirement age, the state-owned company had decided that it would be possible to grant him his pension early, and thus allow him to battle the undiagnosed organic illness without having the worry of considering when it would be possible for him to return to work. In truth, however, Zachary suspected they were relieved not to have him lingering in the news office.

He looked like a corpse already; his once lustrous shock of thick white hair now all fallen out, and his inability to keep food down combined with loss of appetite resulted in a degree of weight loss that was frightening in its rapidity. His joints ached, unsightly purple blotches appeared randomly on his skin, and he had difficulty climbing stairs, or in any form of exercise due to fatigue and shortness of breath.

None of his clothes fitted him properly anymore, all of them being far too large for his emaciated frame, and they hung from his body like the baggy folds of a huge overcoat, one as titanic as an ancient elephant's hide. He disturbed his colleagues, whose displays of sympathy were tinged with the awkwardness that invariably accompanies an ever-present reminder of human mortality, and, since Zachary had no wife or family to support him in his day-to-day life, he imparted to them the details of the suffering he underwent.

An illness that cannot be identified by the medical establishment is an awkward gap, like an unsubstantiated alibi. Though some form of leukaemia was mentioned as a possible explanation, the exact hypothesis was never confirmed.

Had he been at management level it is possible that some advisory or consultative role would have been designed for him; a privilege by way of which he might be partially withdrawn from active participation in business affairs but not entirely removed altogether.

But he had given up all ambitions of management in his early thirties, and had been content to forfeit responsibilities he did not want. He had gradually drifted into becoming the trades-union representative, and had exercised power by way of opposition without responsibility. Though he had long sought the adulation that had been his real aim all along, by this circuitous route, he had not obtained it. His intrinsic bitterness had been too apparent, even to those who were ideologically in sympathy with him. He did not possess any real sympathy for his fellow man, on an individual basis, and tended to divide them into categories, each according to a scale of general characteristics, such as gender, skin colour and degree of disability.

Naturally, with recent cutbacks, the board felt justified in not extending to Zachary any considerations that were not strictly mandatory, and even his 'comrades' were glad to be rid of him, since they had long since seen through his public image. In terms of liberal or leftish politics, his conduct was impeccable, but, when it came to personal relationships, it was a case of him being loved by all, save those who actually knew him.

And it was exactly friendship of those his own age he required, but that was neither a business nor an ideological consideration. He had not earned loyalty or respect, because those qualities were not a feature of his own behaviour.

This situation resulted in his being, through his own efforts, cast adrift amidst much younger and more ambitious staff. Either they resented him and his endless 'do-gooding' or else they did not remain long in the company's employ. It was nigh impossible for him to forge meaningful personal relationships.

That Zachary had lived into an age for which he had little hope – and towards which he was utterly antipathetic – was evident, not least to those members of society with whom he was forced to interact.

The fall of the Berlin Wall had signalled the end of his

hopes for the worldwide adoption of atheistic communism. Those insightful people who detected his disappointment were few in number, but their natural, albeit unconscious, recoil at Zachary's habits and appearance was all the more devastating.

Chiefly, of course, his new personal contacts consisted of interaction with those who attempted to stem and reverse the nameless disease that threatened his life; with the doctors and nurses of the local hospital whence he obtained the debilitating drugs that attempted to kill his mysterious affliction before he himself was killed by the side-effects.

With regards to his body, Zachary had admitted defeat. He had accepted the creed of seeing his existence as merely a materialistic accident of circumstance; and nothing more than the sum total of what a flesh-and-blood being could experience during the course of any individual sojourn in human existence.

This stance had been accentuated by age; for he saw all of the events taking place in the world as being echoes of all those that had taken place before, although in a form differing only according to minor variations in the revolving time sphere.

Wars, famines, earthquakes, floods, massacres, omnipresent from age to age; and were even apparent from the span of a mere fifty-year cycle. The details changed, but the essence was invariably the same. When, as a student in 1968, he had manned the barricades and looked forward gladly to another revolution, one along true Marxist lines, he would have destroyed himself rather than live into an age where religious belief still persisted.

The doctors and nurses all concentrated on his physical well-being, on the extending of the delay in a natural process, since, after all, everyone must die in the end.

Science, Zachary thought, had rightfully replaced God. It had done so mainly by virtue of its holding out the possibility of staving off physical death, by thwarting, for a longer period than hitherto before, what was ultimately inevitable. Science, alone, the vanguard and justifier of materialism, was worthy of respect. It was a force that drove into disarray all those superstitious fools who denied the truth of absolute rationalism.

Zachary did not fear death; for that was mere oblivion, a snuffing out of an insignificant candle-flame, but he feared the pain accompanying the descent into its depths of blackness.

Though he had been a Catholic in youth, he scoffed at the idea of the age of the saints, and their iron faith, for it was many centuries in the past, and now mere legend, if it had ever really existed at all. He laughed at those who still claimed to be believers and who feared they now existed in occupied, enemy territory, in a corrosive secular age opposed to the very idea of the immortal human spirit.

Such an outlandish notion was the cranky preserve of old women with covered heads who knelt in the corner of near-empty churches. A cover for a conspiracy whose aim was to tyrannise over others in the name of a dead God. If there were any answers to the problems confronting humankind they were to be found only in the Marxist solidarity. Anyone who thought otherwise was a victim of false consciousness and deserved to be ostracised. It was a merciful act really, for, in other times, they might well have been shot for the greater good necessitated by the revolution.

Not that Zachary ever voiced these opinions aloud. He had managed to advance his own party agenda, not by being completely open about its aims, but rather by a process of stealth and by discrediting whatever moral authority the reactionary opposition tried to claim.

And he would try not to think these things over and over again at night, when he wished to sleep, but he could not escape the fact that his mind proved most active in those darkest hours. During the day he avoided self-reflection, and drowned himself in books, but learning nothing since he sought out only the ideas of those who confirmed his own viewpoint.

Nevertheless he craved thought-extinguishing sleep at the end of it all, sleep that acted like a blessed narcotic, for it alone blotted out all the worries to which he was prey. When he thought he had conquered the worst of these horrid distractions, and when sleep came more easily, then it was that he began to notice the sounds filtering through the wall separating his apartment from that of the other tenant.

At first he tried to ignore them, but it proved impossible to do so. Over the course of the first week since their advent, he had come to anticipate the distractions and found himself staying awake until they began – always at the same moment, down to the exact second.

It is true that at first they diverted Zachary from his own self-absorption and the nightmares of his own imaginings, but their nature was such that any relief was transitory, for they proved only to be a bridge from one horror to another.

As has been already indicated, the sounds consisted of crackling and static-riddled screaming and moaning, interspersed with lengthy monologues of a macabre and self-accusatory cast. Zachary attempted to jot down some gist of the words he'd heard, but the result was a jumbled mix of almost incomprehensible ravings and filthy expletives.

It is not to be thought that Zachary, during the early part of the manifestation of his problems with his neighbour, did not attempt to put a stop to them. He hammered on the adjoining wall several times, shouted through it, left notes the following morning, and even finally tried knocking on the entrance to the other tenant's apartment at all times of the day and night.

Not once did he receive any response and no change was effected in the maddening routine to which Zachary had become a victim. In moments of paranoia, he suspected the other tenant to be engaged upon a vindictive campaign directed against him personally, but for what end he could not conceive.

He eventually contacted the owner of the building and got a list of all the various sub-owners of the flats into which it had been divided. The owners of the apartment of the other tenant were an estate agency, and when Zachary contacted them his enquiry was met with bewilderment.

They informed him, by letter, that although they took complaints of anti-social behaviour, and especially the type of noise pollution that he described with the utmost seriousness they were also, in this instance, at a loss to know how they could be of any assistance. Their records clearly indicated that the property in question had been unoccupied for several months, and furthermore, that, during the period in which Zachary claimed the trouble had begun, it had remained unleased to any tenant.

Indeed, such was their concern, they had sent a representative almost immediately upon receipt of Zachary's letter in order to investigate any illegal occupancy, and this person had duly gained entrance to the property; but only to report back that there were no signs at all of any squatters or other intruders having gained entrance to the premises.

Given this information, and the lack of any concrete way forward in order to resolve the situation, Zachary decided to take it upon himself to investigate.

He initially hesitated at this course of action, but his agitation and paranoia had reached such a feverish pitch that it was impossible to do anything else. Zachary had passed night after unbearable night lying awake and listening to the audio horrors streaming through the thin gulf between his own and that other apartment, and he was now entirely in the grip of a single obsession; namely, that of discovering the secret behind the dividing wall.

It was not difficult to gain access to the apartment of the other tenant, and Zachary did so one night after yet another interminable period of lying awake and listening yet again to the self-same bloodcurdling broadcasts or recordings to which he had been subjected over the course of the previous weeks. On this particular occasion, he felt, he would either put an end to them once and for all or else go mad from their cumulative effect.

Crossing the landing that separated the entrance to his own apartment from the other, he discovered that its door-frame was rotten with age, and guessed that a shoulder charge would, in all likelihood, make it give way entirely, exposing its locks as more decorative than secure.

So it proved, and despite Zachary's severely weakened state, he found himself forcefully stumbling over the threshold into the confines of that mysterious series of rooms adjoining his own.

The noise he'd heard from his own apartment and which he might have expected to cease upon his arrival was now almost deafening in its intensity.

It emanated from a television set. The device appeared to date from the late 1960s or the early 1970s. The glow from its black and white images filled the empty room with a haze of electric monochrome shadows.

Zachary moved in front of the screen, and sat down in a chair positioned in the middle of the barren room. Next to one of its legs there was a large clawhammer and about thirty nine-inch nails. Though perplexed by the strange debris left behind by whomsoever had occupied the apartment before, Zachary's attention returned to what was being displayed on the screen.

The picture was ruinous, as a result of being imperfectly tuned into the channel on which the images were carried, but he was able to make out the main details despite the interference and snow-bursts of static.

A painfully thin man was imprisoned in an empty room, and seated in a chair. He was gazing at something in abject terror, something currently off-camera, and whatever it was must have been a hideously shocking sight. His features were difficult to distinguish – rendered indistinct by the poor quality of the broadcast, though his crackling screams left no doubt he was gripped by an intolerable sense of anguish.

Zachary was able to tear away his attention from what he saw and heard on the screen long enough to wonder about the machine itself. And in doing so, he was only more horribly astonished. For one thing the television set was not plugged into a power socket. For another, there was no indoor aerial connected to the set, and no connecting cable to provide input for an outside source of transmission. The device seemed entirely self-contained, as if generating from within itself the nightmarish horrors that Zachary was seeing and hearing.

The screams of the man whose image was displayed on the television set both intensified and became punctuated, and Zachary saw that he was using the clawhammer to pierce the flesh of his left arm with the nails, pinning himself to the wooden limb of the chair, and, despite the ferocious agony, not halting in the act of banging them in one after another, this time with his head, and thereby pinning his right arm down too.

When his grisly task was accomplished, the picture closed in on the face of the tortured victim, who was now struggling wildly in the throes of a noxious insanity. His mouth foamed with a black saliva like tar and his eyes bubbled, oozing tears of blood down his pale cheeks.

It was at that moment Zachary found himself staring into his own features, frozen in a grimace of living death, whilst all of the rotten thoughts and all of the hypocrisy, all of the foul deeds and the disloyal lies he'd perpetrated during his life played out on the television screen in the background; in a repetitive and agonisingly slow sequence of endless slow-motion replays.

He reached down for the hammer and the nails, eager to begin the work of spiritual redemption that lay before him.

*

"Yes," the estate agent said, "he died a week ago, choked himself to death, and, probably for some bizarre sexual kick, had nailed himself onto a chair in the vacant and long empty

87

apartment next door. Quite deranged. But he was, after all, terminally ill."

There was no denying the scandal, since it had been reported in all the local newspapers.

"But naturally we're prepared to lower the rent, because we'd rather it was occupied than not."

The prospective tenant nodded and decided to sign the tenancy agreement the estate agent had pulled from the breast pocket of his navy blue pinstriped suit. The prospective tenant had little choice, as he was a declared bankrupt and this was the cheapest accommodation he could find. His career as an author had proven to be a complete financial disaster.

Within a week from the night he moved in he was disturbed by the sound of a television set blaring through the thin, dividing wall. Whoever was responsible for the racket seemed to have a taste for watching nothing but horror films.

TOK

Paul Finch

After they'd hacked and slashed the two bodies for several minutes, they danced on them. The firelight of a dozen torches glittered on their wild, rolling eyes, on their upraised blades, on the blood spattered liberally across the carpet of smoothly mown grass. Their shouts of delight filled the seething night. But when the little girl came out and stood on the veranda, there was a silence like a thunderclap. For a moment she seemed too pure to be in the midst of such mayhem, too angelic – a white-as-snow cherub, who, for all her tears and soiled nightclothes, brought a chill to the muggy forest by her mere presence, brought a hush to the yammering insects, brought the frenzied rage out of her captors like poison from a wound.

If it wasn't the little girl herself, it was the thing she held by her side.

The thing they knew about by instinct.

The thing they'd seen only in nightmares.

*

It was late afternoon when Don and Berni drove onto the estate. Not surprisingly, there were police everywhere: patrol cars parked on the street-corners, uniformed officers traipsing door-to-door with clipboards. Don's blue Nissan Micra was subjected to a stop-and-check.

"Don Presswick," he said, after powering his window down. "This is my wife, Bernadette. We're visiting my mother for a couple of days. She lives at the Grove."

The officer, who was young with fair hair, but wearing a grim expression, gave them a curt once-over. "I don't suppose you've got any ID, Mr Presswick?"

Don didn't have, but Berni rooted in her handbag and

handed over a couple of credit cards. This seemed to satisfy the officer, though he still didn't smile.

He passed the cards back. "You're aware what's been going on?"

"That's why we're here," Don said. "To baby-sit mum 'til it's over."

"Good idea." The officer tapped the roof with his fingers. "Okay, that's fine."

"Listen …" Don adopted a confidential tone. "How's it going? The investigation, I mean. Obviously it's a concern, with my mum living on the estate."

"Sorry Mr Presswick, there's nothing I can tell you."

"I'm ex-job. Don't know if that makes any difference."

The officer shrugged. "I can't tell you anything because I don't know anything. Enquiries are ongoing, as you'll understand. We've a lot of bodies working on it."

Don thanked him and drove on.

"Bloody woodentop," he said.

"*You* were only a PC," Berni reminded him.

"I had a lot more experience than him."

"They all have to start somewhere."

"Suppose so. Just wish it wasn't on mum's estate, at *this* moment."

It was only the third time Berni had visited the Grove since she'd married Don, but again she was reminded how lovely an old property it could be.

A large, five-bedroom detached, built well before the rest of the housing estate, it had been constructed in the Jacobean style – though it was actually Victorian – and was almost entirely clad with white plaster and black beams. Much of this was now weathered, the little you could see of it thanks to the high wall surrounding it, not to mention the tall trees in its front, rear and side gardens. Glimpsed though the red autumn foliage, the plaster had turned green and was flaking; the beams were covered in lichen, those sections that weren't being eaten away by a shroud of crawling ivy. The roofs,

which stood at numerous levels and angles, were also eroding:
crabby with moss, their guttering packed with birds' nests.

"Such a shame," Berni said

"All be yours someday," Don replied, getting out to unlock
the large timber gate.

"Assuming there's anything left of it by then."

Don eased the Micra through, climbed out again and closed
the gate behind them. From here, the drive circled around the
front garden to the rear of the house. Don only had a key for
the back door, so that was where he usually parked. But before
they'd driven more than a couple of yards, the front door
opened and Helga, his mother's cleaner and cook, emerged,
wearing her mackintosh and brandishing her bag. Don applied
the brakes, his tyres crunching gravel.

Helga was a burly woman, with broad, heavy cheekbones.
Her dark hair was shot with grey. Untidy straggles of it hung
loose from the bun at the back of her large, square head. Not
for the first time, Berni wondered why Don's mother, Miriam,
needed a cleaner at all. She lived here alone, in a house that
was patently too large for her, and, despite being wealthy, led a
frugal existence. What there was for Helga to do all day, apart
from cook the occasional meal, was a mystery. No doubt Helga
didn't complain, though it was understandable that she didn't
want to hang around at the Grove now that it was getting dark.
Don and Berni climbed from the car, Berni suggesting quietly
that Don give Helga a ride to the bus stop on the edge of the
estate.

"Thank Heaven!" Helga said brusquely.

She might be employed by Don's mother as a domestic
servant, but she never behaved that way. Quite the opposite.
Her tone seemed to imply how ridiculous it was that they
hadn't been here several hours earlier, though they'd only been
able to leave Stockport once Berni had finished for the day at
the legal firm where she worked as a secretary, and in that
respect had made good time.

"The heating's on and there's plenty of hot water," Helga

said. "I'm afraid I haven't had time to prepare any tea for you."

Don waved it away. "That's fine, we'll just …"

"I'm supposed to be in at nine tomorrow," Helga interrupted. "Though I must tell you I'm not happy, the way things are."

"So … you *won't* be in tomorrow?"

She shrugged. "We'll have to see how it goes."

"Okay … if that's what you want."

"It's hardly what I *want*." Helga let that point hang; again, the implication seemed to be that, if anyone was at fault here, it was Don. "Anyway, I must rush."

She set off down the drive.

"I'm not sure it's as bad as all this," he called after her. She glanced back at him. "What I mean is … there are police officers all over the estate."

"They haven't done much good so far, have they, Mr Presswick?"

And that, Berni supposed, was true. Don had said what he'd said in an effort to suppress the woman's anxiety. But it had been a little crass given that, in the last three nights on this housing estate, three different women had been murdered, and their killer was still on the loose.

"They'll catch him," Don said, rather lamely.

Helga gave him a withering stare in which all the doubts she'd ever had about his knowing anything worthwhile were implicit, before saying: "I'll call Mrs Presswick tomorrow."

She continued down the drive, Don watching her broad back and large, sagging bottom until she'd vanished through the gate.

"I doubt *she's* got much to worry about," he said.

"At least *one* of the victims was middle-aged, wasn't she?" Berni replied.

"Would you try and tackle Helga?"

"I don't think it's funny, Don."

"Neither do I." He climbed into the car and started the

92

engine.

Berni climbed in too. "I thought you were going to drive her to the bus stop?"

"I never agreed to that."

As they prowled around to the rear of the house, Berni said no more on the matter. Don had served as a policeman for the first twelve years of his working life, and as a security officer ever since. Now that he was in his late thirties, he'd gone a little to seed, but he was still a rangy, raw-boned chap, who stood six feet two inches tall. His hair and beard were greying, but he was handsome in a craggy, masculine sort of way. He regarded himself as a man's man, which made it all the more galling for him to have to put up with Helga's domineering manner. Not that this was an unusual experience for him. In many ways, Helga was an extension of his mother and, in that respect, petty victories, like refusing to offer her a ride when she was in a hurry, were the only victories he would ever really have over her.

They entered the house through the kitchen, which was all dark wood panelling with a linoleum floor. Beyond the kitchen lay the dining room, the hall and the lounge. It was all very tidy, but throughout the furnishing and décor were sombre and old fashioned. The rooms were tall, with elaborate, hand-painted cornicing around their ceilings, but there were heavy curtains drawn everywhere, which made the house's interior dim to the point where it was almost difficult to find one's way around. Carpets and rugs, many threadbare and frayed, muffled all sound as Don and Berni entered the lounge. There was scarcely a peep from the outside world. The windows, which were double-glazed, were presumably closed and locked. The walls of this house were very thick, and then of course there was the tree-filled garden encircling it, and the high wall encircling the garden.

Thanks to the radiator in each room, the house was warm, as Helga had said, but it felt stuffy and lived-in. The air smelled stale. Berni gazed at her reflection in the large mirror hanging over the stone fireplace; thanks to its deeply tarnished glass, only a fogged spectre gazed back. When she ran a fingertip along the top of the mantel, it drew a visible trail. Don made no comment when she mentioned this. Instead, he grabbed their two holdalls – his blue-grey in colour, hers covered with pink flower-patterns – and took them up the steep, creaking staircase to the first floor.

Berni glanced around, as always, irritated by the steady process of neglect that continued to reduce her husband's nest egg to a pathetic shadow of what it once must have been. Upstairs, she heard the strident tones of Don's mother, as she berated him for not getting here sooner.

Miriam Presswick had not always lived like a hermit in her own home. When the Grove had been the sole dwelling on this broad, green Lancashire hillside, with only a clutch of trees to shelter it from the heather-scented breeze of the Pennines, she had, for a time, come out of the mental exile that she'd lived in since returning to England from Africa, and enjoyed life again. Even after her husband's premature death, she'd made an effort to remain in the real world. Inevitably though, the nearest town – Layburn, once three miles away – had continued to expand, and by the mid-1980s one of its multiple new housing estates, 'the Bannerwood', had engulfed the one-time country house. The Bannerwood wasn't by any means a 'problem' housing estate, being privately owned and suburban in character. But it was vast and sprawling, and on first being built it was occupied mainly by young families, which soon meant there were lots of children running around – so many children, as Miriam Presswick would complain. Children in gangs, children running, children shouting, children screaming – and children encroaching, always encroaching, finding ever more reasons to trespass on her property: in summer chasing footballs or playing hide and seek among her trees, in autumn trick-or-treating or throwing fireworks onto her lawn.

Berni didn't know whether such persecutions had actually taken place or were purely imaginary, but given Miriam's personal history it was no surprise that her sense of embattlement had finally become so acute that she'd had the outer wall erected, cutting herself off completely from the busy world that had suddenly encircled her. Despite that, but not atypically of psychological breakdown (not to mention advancing senility), even this security measure had in due course proved insufficient. In the last year alone, Miriam had contacted her son on average once a week to complain that people were trying to climb over the wall, were scratching on her doors, tapping on her windows. Nonsense, of course. Utter nonsense. Though Don had not admitted that. He would never have the guts to be so abrupt with his mother. He'd tried to calm her, tried to reassure her that she was imagining it – to no avail.

And then, this last week, the murders had started.

Berni only knew what she'd read in the papers, but on three consecutive nights an unknown assailant had entered homes on the Bannerwood estate and strangled a woman to death in each one. It was pretty difficult to take Miriam's fears with a pinch of salt under those circumstances.

Don now came downstairs. As always after a meeting with his mother, he looked chastised.

"She okay?" Berni asked.

"She's fine."

"Happy?"

"Happier." Though he didn't look as if he was being entirely truthful with that. "Don't suppose you fancy popping to the chippie and bringing us something for tea?"

"Sure." Berni had taken her coat off, but now pulled it on again.

"Hang on." He raised a hand. "*You'd* better not go. I'll go."

"It's okay. It's not even dark yet."

"It's getting dark."

"Don, there are coppers all over the estate."

"Yeah, and like Helga said, what bloody good have they been?"

Tok

Berni took her coat off again. She wasn't usually so quick to follow her husband's orders. A born and bred Scouser, 'toughness' and 'independence' were her two middle names. But there was something about visiting the Grove that she found oppressive. Its brooding aura, not to mention the aura of its queenly owner, always seemed to sap her energy to resist. She wondered if this was the spell the aristocracy had woven in olden times, when an awed peasantry made them superior simply by believing that they were. Miriam was no aristocrat of course, but she had been raised among the colonial classes.

"What are you having?" Don said, lurching along the hall.

"Fish and chips is fine. Bring us a buttered barm as well."

He nodded and left, the heavy oak door clicking closed behind him.

Berni found herself alone in deepening gloom. There was something she could do about *that* at least – she opened the curtains in the lounge. Thanks to the crowded trees outside, it didn't improve things much, so she switched various lamps on. Their shades were exclusively of heavy, tasselled material, which seemed more designed to absorb light than release it. In the kitchen, she took dishes from the sideboard and cutlery from a drawer. She filled the kettle and put tea bags into a pair of mugs. She then prepared for what was always going to have been the most difficult duty of the night: saying 'hello' to Miriam. She halted at the foot of the stairs. Two thirds of the way up, there was a small sub-landing, where the stair turned right. That too had a curtained window. When Berni reached it, she pondered the wisdom of opening this curtain as well. Miriam wouldn't like it, but Miriam was becoming less capable by the day, and maybe it was time people realised that – especially Miriam herself.

Feeling justified, Berni jerked the drape back along its brass rod – and yelped aloud when she saw the ugly shape hiding behind it.

Perhaps 'hiding' was too strong a term.

It was only a figurine, which had been mounted on a wooden

base and placed in the recessed alcove in front of the narrow, stained-glass window. That said, it was easily the most repulsive thing that Berni had ever seen.

It was about three feet tall, and though it stood upright on two legs, her first thought was that it was a stuffed chimpanzee or some other kind of ape. It had coarse hair all over its body, and was now shrivelled and dry. But there was nothing quaint or ornamental about it. Its eyes were empty sockets, while its mouth had been fixed in a snarl that split its head from ear to ear, and in which two rows of thorns had been placed to provide fangs. Though its posture was stooped and its knees bent, certain of its features were more humanoid than anthropoid.

Berni wondered what on earth she was looking at.

The sides of the creature's torso and the undersides of its thin, gangling arms were not hairy, but covered with dark, leathery skin. Likewise its face: its nostrils flared, its sloped brow was furrowed as though by intense concentration. The hair began again on top of its small, anvil-shaped head, but it was short and spiky, deliberately caked with what looked like dried clay – combined with those hollow eye-sockets, this was perhaps the most hideous aspect of the thing, because it suggested a degree of intelligence.

Intelligence? What the devil was she thinking? Surely this mannequin had been *made*. A creature like this could never have actually lived. It had to be a mock-up.

Berni seemed to remember that Miriam had purposely divested herself of all the relics from her time in Africa. Yet this thing bespoke not just Africa, but *darkest* Africa, *savage* Africa. Maybe it was a joke. Perhaps comic creations like this were on sale at every market stall from Banjul to Johannesburg. Though, in truth, there was nothing comical about the necklace the mannequin wore, which looked to be composed of human teeth, while its small leather thong, the frontal pouch of which apparently contained a small set of male genitals, was surely taking realism a touch too far. The alcove, while whitewashed, had been marked with red and blue paint in what looked like tribal symbols: abstract patterns, pictographs of animals and hunters, and crude glyphs, which, now that she looked closely, might signify some kind of writing …

"Don't you dare touch that!" came a sharp voice.

Berni spun around.

Miriam gazed imperiously down from the top of the next flight. She was a tall woman, but her emaciated figure did not benefit from this. Nor from her flowing nightgown. A diaphanous garment, all ruffles and lace, on Miriam it hung baggy and shapeless. Despite being in her bed-wear, she wore make-up – there'd never been a time when Berni hadn't seen Miriam wearing make-up – but now the effect was grotesque, because the woman was so cadaverous. She'd kept her hair long, but where it had once been auburn, it was now grey and hung past her shoulders in rat-tails. Miriam was not old – at a conservative estimate no more than sixty-five. But her deteriorated condition was a testament to the self-imposed stress she'd suffered over the years.

"Oh, Bernadette … forgive me." Miriam had lived in Lancashire since returning to England in the 1950s, but unlike her late husband, a local factory owner, who she'd met after moving here, and unlike her son, who'd been born and raised here, she'd never developed an accent. Her voice was 'BBC' neutral. "Forgive me," she said again, still not sounding as if she meant it. "I didn't recognise you."

Berni didn't believe that. If Miriam had found someone she thought she didn't know on the staircase in her house, she'd have had a fit. But now was not the time for a fight.

"Well … we haven't seen each other for a while," Berni said. "How are you, Miriam?"

"How are any of us … in *this* place?"

"I'm sorry about the curtain. I was just trying to let some light in."

"I'd rather keep the curtains drawn."

"I don't blame you in this case." Berni indicated the mannequin. "What's this?"

"You haven't seen him before?" Miriam sounded surprised. "That's Tok."

Tok? Such an inoffensive name for something so repellent.

"Would you mind closing that curtain, dear?" Miriam had the ability to make any request into a thinly veiled command.

Berni did so.

"And where is Donald?" Miriam asked.

"He's gone to get us some tea."

"I see. I'd hoped he'd be spending the next few nights here. But apparently he can't."

"He's got to go to work. But *I'll* be here."

Miriam's attempted half-smile indicated that only politeness prevented her saying what she felt about *this* part of the arrangement. "Buying tea is very thoughtful," she said, "but you needn't have bothered on my behalf. I'm not at all hungry. Please send Donald up when he returns. I'd like to speak with him again."

"Of course, I'll …"

But the conversation was over. Miriam perambulated out of sight. Berni went downstairs and into the lounge. She surveyed the sombre room that would be her home for the next few days. If the police hadn't caught the killer by that time, she'd need a serious talk with Don about what they were going to do. They had lives to lead, after all. Speaking of which – she picked the hand-control up and switched the television on, settling on a news channel that was coming live from somewhere on the Bannerwood.

A crime-reporter in an overcoat and scarf was standing under arc lights in front of an outside-broadcast caravan. "All we know is that the police have not ruled out burglary as a possible motive," he said.

The anchorwoman, a pretty blonde, who looked suitably concerned by the string of dreadful events, asked, "Have the police commented further on the *modus operandi* of these murders, Dylan? We've heard rumours that the three victims were strangled, though we've had no confirmation."

"The police aren't commenting, though there is a press conference lined up for tomorrow morning. I expect we'll learn more …"

Berni switched to another channel. Here, a group of people, this time inside a studio, were also discussing the crisis. Having few actual facts to hand, the presenter was allowing the conversation to range freely.

"I think we're all getting a bit sick and tired of the objectification of women!" This came from an elderly lady in a smart skirt suit and dangly earrings, who Berni thought was a famous author. "These gossip magazines are full of female celebrities wearing next to nothing, or talking endlessly about their sex lives, which are nearly always lurid and scandalous. We've got girl bands dressing like Times Square hookers; we've got schoolgirls copying them when they go out to discos and nightclubs …"

"I think you could argue that men are being objectified as well," a male guest replied. He too was elderly and wore a smart suit; Berni recognised him as an editor in the tabloid press. "If you look at the world of pornography …"

"Well, you ought to know about the world of pornography, Tarquin," the author interrupted. "Your newspaper has done its best to promote that industry, along with the breast enhancement industry, and the stockings and suspenders and see-through knickers industries …"

"Perhaps we're moving off the point," the presenter said hastily. "We shouldn't forget the three victims."

"*I'm* not forgetting them," the newspaper editor replied, "but I think Sheila's running before her horse to market. The police haven't even confirmed that these were sex attacks."

"Oh come on!" the author protested.

"I wasn't aware that you were an expert on deviant psychology, Sheila. To start with, look at the age-ranges of the victims. The oldest was fifty-eight, while the other two were

100

thirty and nineteen respectively. That's an unusual variation of victim-types for a traditional serial killer. If anything, what we're dealing with here is a spree killer …"

"Serial killer, spree killer … women are being slaughtered, and Tarquin's talking semantics."

"*Sheila!* Sensationalist language will not help."

"Sensationalist language is all we've got, Tarquin. In houses all over the Bannerwood estate, which in case you've forgotten is only seventeen miles from the studio here in Manchester, there are women watching this programme, wondering if tonight will be the night when some drink-sodden animal forces his way through their downstairs window, sneaks up to their bedroom and inflicts God knows what kind of atrocities on them …"

Berni flicked the television off.

For the first time it really struck her what it was that Don had asked her to do here. She hadn't been happy about rooming at the Grove for all sorts of obvious reasons, but it had never occurred to her until now that, in consenting to do this, she might not just be risking attack herself, but *inviting* it.

Berni had always wrapped men round her little finger. She was slim and petite, but also shapely – a figure she'd maintained despite having reached her mid-thirties. She had dark, bobbed hair and sultry Italian looks. Even back in her teenage years, when surrounded by braying drunks in city centre bars, she'd never felt a hint of danger from them, because, with a word or gesture, she could reduce them to lumps of slobbering jelly. But perhaps in agreeing to do *this*, she'd taken that self-assurance a little too far.

She moved to the window.

It was now dark outside. All she could see were the boles of the nearest trees, and drifts of fallen leaves between them. Beyond those, thanks to the garden wall, there was only blackness, though one or two twinkles of yellow streetlight showed over the top. She closed the curtain, not wanting anyone to see that a lone woman was peeking out.

101

Something rattled in the hall.

At first Berni thought nothing of it, but then she froze. It had sounded like the front door. Had someone just tried to get in? She listened intently, but heard nothing else. Most likely it had been a gust of wind.

Except that she couldn't leave it at that.

She walked into the hall. The front door was only ten feet away, but suddenly that didn't feel far enough. Was it possible, she wondered – was someone on the other side, his ear pressed against the wood. She advanced warily. The door's lock engaged automatically when the door closed, so it should be secure, though she noticed that the safety-chain was hanging loose. That was the solution. All she had to do was fix the chain, open the door a crack and glance out. And yet how many horror movies had she seen where that had never been enough, where at the first chink of light the powerhouse maniac had forced his way through?

"Un-bloody-believable!" came a loud voice behind her.

Berni twirled around, her heart skipping a beat.

Don was standing in the doorway to the kitchen, holding a plastic carrier bag stuffed with paper parcels; there was a sudden aroma of vinegar.

"You'd think folk'd be too scared to go out," he said. "But there must have been twenty in that queue."

"Please tell me you just tried the front door."

He looked nonplussed. "Why would I? I haven't got a key for it."

"Someone just has."

Don hurried to the door and yanked it open. There was no one outside, but the breeze was stiffening. Curled leaves danced through the darkness. He pointed this out. It made sense, though Berni was still grateful when the door was closed again. She led the way through to the kitchen, where the plates and cutlery were waiting.

"Mum not down yet?" Don asked.

"I doubt she's coming down," Berni said, dishing up. "She

took one look at me and decided she didn't have an appetite."

Don nodded as if this, while not understandable, was at least forgivable – a mute acquiescence to his parent's unreasonable attitude, which exasperated Berni more than she could say.

"You know, Don … this is not an easy thing you've asked me to do."

"I know that."

"It might have been more helpful if *you'd* taken a few days off work, instead of me."

"I've tried to explain that the short-notice thing wasn't possible with *our* rosters."

"Maybe you should explain it to your mum when you go back up. She wants another word."

He nodded resignedly. "Okay. I'll not be long."

"You reckon?"

Of course, Don was quite some time upstairs. Berni found a tray, and ate her fish and chips from her knee in the lounge, the TV news at last having given way to *The Simpsons*, though in reality she was listening to the raised voices upstairs, or rather the raised *voice*. No doubt, Don would be offering the same solutions to their usual intractable problem, and Miriam would be rebuffing them in the same old way. If they sold their respective homes, he'd be arguing, they could pool their resources and buy a house together. Miriam wouldn't hear of it (and thank God for that, Berni thought). Well, why didn't Miriam sell up and move into sheltered accommodation? She wouldn't be alone and would have good security. Again, Miriam would refuse, saying that *this* was her home and that she would never abandon it to the forces of chaos outside. But if she was frightened, Don would protest … Anyone would be frightened, Miriam would reply. But *she* was made of sterner stuff.

When he finally came downstairs, he looked even more chastened than before.

"Yours has gone cold," Berni said. "I'd stick it in the microwave, but your mum doesn't have one."

"It's alright."

"I can put the oven on, but it'll take a while."

"I haven't got time for that."

"You're going to work already?"

"Well, it's an extra forty minutes from here, isn't it?"

Berni glanced at her watch: it was just past six. "Are the coppers still outside?"

"They're all over the estate."

That wasn't really answering the question. Though Berni knew that even if a police car was parked up on the other side of the garden wall, it wouldn't stay there all night.

"I've put the bags in the third bedroom," he said. "Want to come and check we've got everything?"

They went upstairs together. The landing, like the staircase, was dark and creaky. The only light up there filtered around the door from Miriam's bedroom. Berni wondered what it was like inside: no doubt ornate though again faded and filmed with dust; Miriam would be laid out in the midst of it like some aged, ailing movie star.

Their own room was more basic. It contained all the necessaries: a wardrobe, a side-table with a nightlight on it, and of course a double bed made up with clean bedding. Berni peeked around the curtain. From up here, she could look down through largely leafless branches, and was able to see over the perimeter wall. She surveyed the neighbourhood. It was a little cluttered maybe, but it was firmly middle-class compared to the housing estate she'd grown up on in Liverpool. The houses were tidy – some were semis, some were detached. They all had gardens, and cars or caravans on their drives. There wasn't as much police activity as there had been, though a panda car was parked on the adjacent road. Its driver was talking to a helmeted foot-patrol, who, shortly afterwards, moved away, saying something into his radio before vanishing around a corner. She glanced further afield, trying not to notice the shadowed passages between vehicles and houses, or the black spots behind bushes where someone could be lurking.

"What time will you be back?" she asked, as Don buttoned up his grey uniform.

"Same as usual. Sevenish."

"It won't be the same as usual, will it? You're forty minutes further away."

"Okay, seven-forty-ish. What does it matter? You'll still be in bed." He zipped his windbreaker, then grabbed his shoulder bag and torch, leaned down and kissed her on the cheek. "I'm off."

They went downstairs together.

"Just out of interest," Berni said as they passed the curtained alcove, "have you seen the vile thing your mum keeps behind there?"

"Oh that, yeah." Don chuckled. "Tok."

"I'm not surprised she has problems living here with that thing."

"You must be joking. Tok's her best mate. She wouldn't be without him."

"Weird bloody name."

They reached the bottom, where Don pulled his gloves on. "Apparently, it's short for Tokoloshe. I don't know what that is. Some kind of good luck charm. You know her dad was a diplomat in Southern Rhodesia. Well, when she was a kid she had a Zulu nurse called Jana, who doted on her. Later, when her dad was transferred to Kenya, Jana was broken-hearted. She gave Tok to mum as a goodbye present. During the Mau Mau rebellion – that's when my grandparents were murdered, and mum was taken hostage – she kept it with her all the time. I suppose it was the only friend she had. When British troops rescued her, she wouldn't give it up for love nor money. Kept it ever since."

"It's still hideous."

He chuckled again. "It's a doll. There must be scabby old dolls folk are sentimental about all over the country. Anyway …" He leaned down and kissed her again.

She resisted the urge to grab him and hug him. He *had* to go to work; there was no choice in the matter. She closed the door, and listened as the crunch of his boots on the gravel faded. A few moments later, she heard the engine at the side of the house. Then that too faded. She went back into the lounge, glancing at her watch. It would be nine hours before he was back. On the TV, *The Simpsons* had finished and a news update was again discussing the murders. A noted crime-writer had now arrived in the studio.

"Despite there not being a home-defence industry in the UK, house invasion murders of this sort are quite rare," he said. "Of course, we're not sure how the killer entered these three premises – the police haven't told us yet – but it's a bit worrying given that most householders these days are sensible about security ..."

Berni wondered if Don had locked the back door when he'd come in earlier. She dashed through to the kitchen, and found the door closed but unlocked.

"Bloody security guards," she said, turning the key.

From somewhere outside there was a metallic clatter. It sounded like the dustbins.

She tried to peer through the glass panel, but it was frosted and revealed nothing. On the back door there was no safety-chain, so when she opened it, she positioned her body behind it in order to throw her full weight against it should she need to.

There was nobody out there. The dustbins stood where they had before, in a row on the other side of the parking space, the emptiness of which only served to remind Berni that Don had gone. One of the dustbin lids appeared to have fallen off. Beyond the bins, leaves swirled through the darkness. The wind was picking up steadily. It might be sufficient to have dislodged the lid.

Berni closed the door and locked it again, before going back into the lounge. She turned the volume down on the television, took her mobile from her pocket and punched in the number of her best friend, Laura.

"Hi babes," Laura said. "Is it absolutely awful?"

"Not *absolutely*," Berni replied, curling up on the sofa. "Miriam's her usual self. The only good thing I can say is that she's gone to bed early."

"They're saying on the news that he's deranged."

"They wouldn't have to be experts to work that out, would they?"

"No, there's a difference." Laura, though a hairdresser by trade, was married to a chap called Neil, who was a forklift truck driver but also an amateur ghost-watcher. The pair of them had what some might call an abnormal interest in the odd and ghoulish, and were mines of useless if creepy information. "If you're officially *deranged*, it means you've got no self-control. That's different from your traditional sex killers, who hunt for victims carefully. If you're *deranged* ..." she enunciated the word lovingly, "it's like you see in the movies, where you just go from house to house, knocking everyone off."

"Love, I don't suppose we can talk about something else?"

"Oh sorry, babes."

Soon they were nattering contentedly – about old friends, about new friends, about work prospects, about social events they wanted to organise, and so on. It was almost nine before Berni noticed the battery light flashing.

"Gotta go, darling," she said. "Wish I could stay on longer."

"Understand. Night, babes."

Once she'd cut the call, Berni plugged the phone into a socket, and stood in front of the TV. There was still no volume, which made the house seem even quieter than before. Perhaps this was why the long, low creak she suddenly heard overhead made her jump.

She went back to the bottom of the stairs, and again paused to listen – nothing.

Ascending, she stopped every few treads, but still heard nothing else. When she reached the top landing, she glanced from one open doorway to the next. All were in darkness, except for Miriam's; her door was still closed and spilling lamplight around its edges. It seemed certain that what Berni had just heard was her mother-in-law pottering around, but the silence from that bedroom now was unnerving.

"Hello?" Berni said, tapping on the door. There was no response. She glanced again at the other darkened doorways. "Miriam … it's me. Can I come in?"

Again there was no reply, so Berni pushed the door gently. It swung open, and she peeked around. The bedroom was much as she'd imagined: a remnant of something once grand. There were even oil paintings in there, and fine brocade: but all of it had seen better days. The carpet was worn; the room's high corners were furred with dust. Piles of unwashed clothes lay everywhere, even across the foot of the bed, where there was also a sewing-box, which had shed several needles, pins and a large pair of shears. A sideboard was jumbled with medicines and bottles of tablets. Miriam was asleep – but not reclined on some four-poster with faded film star elegance; instead, she was curled beneath a thin, patched eiderdown, breathing softly but regularly, her ratty grey hair strewn over a pillow that was stained yellow.

Berni retreated again and closed the door. It was difficult to imagine that Miriam had been walking around in the last few minutes. In which case, what had she heard up here? A floorboard? Sure. But floorboards didn't creak on their own. She pivoted around, watching the other doorways, her hand reaching for the landing light switch. When her phone suddenly trilled downstairs, she almost shouted.

"What've you been doing?" Don said when she answered. "I've been trying to get you all evening."

"Talking to Laura."

"I thought it would be something stupid like that."

"Hey … I'm sorry it was inconvenient. But I'm here on my own, remember? Or I might as well be. Why didn't you try the landline?"

"I didn't want to disturb mum."

"That figures."

"Listen Bern … I think I may have left the back door unlocked earlier."

"You did. I've sorted it."

"Thank God. Check everywhere else is locked as well. I mean *everywhere*." He sounded more anxious than he had done earlier. "I'm going to try and get tomorrow night off after all. And the night after that, if possible."

"Why? What's changed?"

He hesitated, before saying: "I was driving off the estate earlier, and who should I see talking to a couple of uniforms but Les McAllister."

"Weren't you in the job with him?"

"Yeah, he's still in. He's in CID now. I stopped and had a chat. I told him my mum lived here and that you were baby-sitting, and he said, 'Rather you than me, mate.' Berni … these murders, they're not just bad, they're seriously weird."

"Why?" Berni was almost afraid to ask, but suddenly she *had* to know more.

"According to Les, they don't even know how he's getting into the houses. There've been no broken locks or anything like that. There's also no sign that he was let in. The murders happened late at night, when everyone was in bed."

"Maybe he was in already – you know, hiding?"

"They've considered that, but they don't think so. There's *some* evidence … I mean, it sounds crazy."

"Go on," she said nervously.

"At one house, an upper window panel was open."

"Well obviously that's how he got in."

"If he did, he'd have to have been some kind of circus rubber man. Or extremely small."

"Small?"

"The gap was tiny. There were similar things at the other two houses – a cat-flap jammed open, a skylight no bigger than a shoebox. But listen, in this case small doesn't mean weak. Berni, he made a hell of a mess of these women. There were no sexual assaults, but they were brutally strangled, their necks totally busted. And he didn't half pulverize their faces trying to get their teeth out."

"Their teeth?"

"He's collecting trophies."

Clammy hands were all over Berni's skin. "Their *teeth?*"

"He pounded their jaws to pieces. I hope to Heaven it was post-mortem."

"*Oh my God ...*"

"I know." Don clearly assumed the horror he could detect in his wife's voice was a natural reaction to such terrible revelations. "And he's efficient too. I mean, there were other people in the houses. The old dear had two of her daughters living with her, and a couple of her grandkids. None of them heard anything. The thirty-year-old's husband was away, but her three kids were in the next room and they weren't disturbed. The nineteen-year-old was a single mum of two, but they were in ..."

"*Don, just shut up!*"

"What?"

"It's ridiculous ..."

"I agree." They were still talking at cross-purposes. "I'm sorry I've put you in this predicament, love. I can't leave now though. I'm the only man on site, but I'm definitely putting in for some emergency leave tomorrow ..."

"Don, listen to me ..."

"Sorry, love, I've got to go. There's a lorry at the gate." He hung up.

Berni went back up the stairs slowly, with a sense of the unreal. When she reached the first landing, she hardly dared pull the curtain aside.

When she finally found the courage, the Tokoloshe gazed malignly at her with its rotted, empty pits. She presumed it was her imagination that it had changed position. Previously, its arms had been by its sides. Now they seemed to have been raised a little. Even in the darkness, she was better able to see its hands, which were disproportionately large and had long,

110

crooked fingers with black hooks for nails. The temptation was to prod it, to try and discover what it was made from. It was only a doll, she assured herself, but she didn't even want to get close to it, much less reach out and touch the necklace of teeth to find out if the dark stains at their jagged bases might actually be blood.

"Babes!" she shouted into her phone when she got back downstairs. "Tell me everything you know about the Tokoloshe."

"What?" Laura sounded half-asleep.

"Neil must have books or files, or something."

"Berni, what's this about?"

Berni didn't want to tell them the whole story. Even Neil and Laura would think her a lunatic, so she invented a tale about reading a novel and being puzzled by a reference to a mysterious African creature called the Tokoloshe.

"Alright," Laura said grudgingly. "I was in bed, but we've got *some* books with stuff like that. Ring you back in five."

Berni had no sooner hung up than she heard another noise upstairs: a dull, metallic clunk followed by a distinct *scratching-scratching* sound. When she went back into the hall this time, she kept the phone with her, though it could only have been recharged to give her a few extra minutes.

Again, there was only darkness and silence at the top of the stairs.

She climbed stealthily. At the top, Miriam's door was closed. When she tapped on it, there was no response. When she pushed it open, she saw Miriam lying in exactly the same position as before. Again, Berni backed onto the landing. She knew she'd heard something. Most likely there was a humdrum explanation, but she still felt horribly scared, and after what Don had said on the phone, not a little bewildered.

That was when she happened to glance down to the lower landing – and saw the alcove curtain twitch.

Ice spread through her veins.

The curtain twitched again.

Tok

When Berni finally descended to it, there was scarcely a breath in her body. She didn't *want* to do this, but she had no option – she had to get close to the curtain just to pass it. But she was going to look behind it as well, because a morbid fascination dictated that she must. This could not be what she feared. It could *not*. There *had* to be a rational explanation. She was directly in front of the curtain when the phone trilled in her pocket. Wordlessly, she put it to her ear.

"I presume it's a horror novel," Laura said cheerfully. "Because check this out." She began to read, "'A small humanoid being of tribal African mythology. The Tokoloshe is still widely feared in rural parts of Zambia, Zimbabwe, Mozambique and, most specifically, the Kwa-Zulu-Natal province of South Africa. The Tokoloshe is said to have never lived a natural life, but to have been constructed by a shaman, usually from the body parts of other creatures, in order to cause harm to his enemies. Though childlike in stature, it is believed capable of terrible destruction … '"

Laura's voice fizzled away as the phone's half-charged battery gave out.

Berni didn't care. With a pale, sweaty hand, she took hold of the curtain.

… they were brutally strangled, their necks totally busted.

She drew the material back.

The wooden dais was empty. Tok was nowhere to be seen, which was a monumental relief. Though of course this didn't last. The stained glass window stood ajar. Berni peered numbly at its scrolled iron handle, which no doubt had made a *scratching-scratching* sound as it had been turned. Another breeze blew in, causing the curtain to twitch. She retreated in a daze. When a curved claw alighted on her shoulder, she gave a hoarse shriek before spinning around.

Miriam was standing one step above her, her hooked hand still proffered.

"For three nights it went on," the old woman said, her eyes like yellowed marbles as she stared without blinking into a distant, dreadful past. "Noises in the bush around our home. Harsh voices, cruel laughter. Mother was terrified. Father tried to calm her. He said there were squatters on our land. It was inevitable after the deprivations suffered by the Kikuyu. But he knew there'd be oath-takers among them. That's why he loaded his gun, why he battened the windows at night and locked all the doors …"

"Miriam …" Berni tried to interrupt, but Miriam clutched at her, sinking rheumatic fingers into her shoulder.

"By the third day our servants had fled," she said with a shudder. "Mother begged father to send for help. We were only a few miles outside Nairobi, but it was too late. By then the Emergency was in full swing. The police and soldiers were spread too thinly. That third night they finally attacked, banging at our windows and doors with their pangas and machetes. Screaming the most terrible threats. Father shot a couple of them, but that enraged them more. When they dragged him and mother outside … *oh my God, I saw it … from my bedroom window …*"

Again, Berni tried to speak. "Miriam … ?"

But Miriam merely tightened her grip, her eyes glistening with tears, yet her mouth twisted into a strange stiff smile. "I was alone after that. Except … except for Tok. Mother had hated him from the moment Jana gave him to me. She'd wanted father to burn him, but I'd pleaded with her not to. Jana had said he would protect me if I kept him close. In the end, mother had allowed me to keep him so long as he was locked in the cupboard. Well … now I took him out again."

"Miriam …"

"When they came into my room, they were in a fury. Drunk, shrieking. They always shrieked when they were about to kill you. But then they saw Tok, and in one go the anger left them – suddenly *they* were the ones who were afraid." Miriam's smile became a grimace. "They hung back until one of their captains came in. He pointed a gun at me and ordered me outside, but he didn't touch me. I tried not to look at mother

113

and father's bodies as they marched me into the bush. They weren't shrieking any more. They were mumbling, muttering … like the simple-minded peasants they were. Deep in the bush, they put me in a hut and lit a fire outside. They talked all night. I was only nine years old, but I knew *Swahili*. I heard what they were saying. They wanted to kill me too. But now they didn't dare. Two of them, KAU members who had been imprisoned by the Colonial Government and were unimpressed with folk tales, said *they* would do it, and that they would do it quickly in honour of my youth and innocence. Their captain was slowly being swayed, but it was late and he decided they would talk more in morning. But when morning came, those KAU men were dead, their throats torn, their necks broken. And whereas before I had kept my arms around Tok, now his arms were around me … and so they remained for the next six months, while I was a captive, and all that time I was never mistreated. They fed me, clothed me. Didn't dare try to separate me from my protector."

Several seconds passed before Berni realised that Miriam had finished. The older woman treated her daughter-in-law to a beatific smile.

"Miriam, what in God's name … ?"

"Tok knows everything I know, Bernadette. He fears everything I fear. And as these good-for-nothing people, prolific as cockroaches, have come to besiege us once again …"

"Miriam, no one has besieged you!"

"It is happening just as it happened before. But this time the outcome will be different."

Berni shook her head. "Miriam … you surely don't believe this insanity."

"Of course I do, dear. And so do you. A self-centred creature like you wouldn't doubt her own senses."

"Then if it's true, call him back."

Miriam's smile became scornful. "You stupid, foolish girl! I can't call him back. This is *juju* … a curse. It can only be lifted by the sorcerer who invoked it."

"If you won't stop it, the police will." Berni decided she'd heard enough. She headed downstairs. "They're out there somewhere."

"You'd be advised not to side against us, Bernadette. Tok won't like it."

"I'm siding with no one. I'll just tell them what you told me."

Miriam laughed. "And will they believe that … will they believe the word of poor old eccentric Mrs Presswick."

Berni reached the bottom, and glared back up. "They won't need to. When that monster of yours returns, I'll show it to them … I'll show them the teeth it's been collecting." Miriam's smile slowly faded. "They may not believe Tok's the perpetrator, but they'll know that *someone* in this house is. They may decide that poor eccentric Mrs Presswick is a touch *too* eccentric." Berni fiddled with the front door lock. "You may finish in a psychiatric ward, Miriam. Unless they look at Don, of course … he does *everything* mummy tells him, after all!"

Miriam looked stunned. She tottered downstairs. "You traitorous little …"

The door swung open, and Berni hurried out. "And it wouldn't be a hospital for *him!*"

"You'd endanger your own husband!" Miriam shrieked from the doorway.

It was so dark in the enclosed garden that, rather than thread through the trees to the main gate, Berni opted to follow the drive around. Even so, she stumbled a couple of times, and when she reached the gate, she found she had another problem. The gate could only be opened from the other side with a key, of which Don had a copy on his key ring. On the garden side it was a simple latch, but in this depth of darkness she fumbled futilely.

There was a loud thump as the front door was closed.

Berni glanced around. The trees were jet-black stanchions

framed on the gloomy outline of the house. The few leaves left on their interlaced branches blotted out the stars.

She gave up with the gate and took the phone from her pocket – but it was still dead. A hint of movement dragged her attention to the parapet of the north wall.

Had something just vaulted over the top of it?

You'd be advised not to side against us, Bernadette.

Berni felt a chill down her spine, which had nothing to do with the dank wind. She walked back towards the house, this time veering between the trees rather than taking the longer distance around the drive. All the time she scanned the open spaces between herself and the north wall. They were buried in blackness. Something could be creeping towards her, and she wouldn't see it until the last second. Her nerve broke, and she ran the remaining twenty yards, banging loudly on the door.

"Miriam! *Miriam!*"

"Today is a special day, Bernadette," came Miriam's response, sounding hollow and muffled. She must be standing just on the other side.

"Miriam, please!" Berni glanced over her shoulder; there were all kinds of scurryings and rustlings as the wind lashed the leaves.

"Today is October twentieth … Heroes Day, on which the Kenyan people honour their so-called 'freedom fighters'. Through the waning of every year I've watched this date approach with trepidation. But not this year. This year, I decided, it would be different. This year *we* will be the ones to mark Heroes Day. Tok and I. And we will take a fearsome toll …"

"Miriam, let me in!"

But Miriam was no longer there. Berni listened with disbelief as footsteps dwindled away into the house. She swung around to face the garden, her thoughts racing. She could scream and shout. If there were any police in the vicinity they might hear, but that was unlikely given the wind. The back door was locked, as were all the ground-floor windows.

But then she remembered the alcove window. That should still be open.

She darted for the corner of the building, certain that a shapeless blot detached itself from the darkness close by and came hurrying in pursuit. Suppressing squeals of terror, she scrambled around the exterior, clattering through the dustbins, spilling their contents – even grabbing up a lid and hurling it behind her – until she sighted the stained glass portal. It *was* still open. What was more, an apron of luxuriant ivy descended beneath it.

Berni began to climb – hand over hand, refusing to look down. Clumps of vegetation tore loose in her hands, but she was of slight build, and it held. Soon, she was on level with the window. Still refusing to look down, she hefted her right leg over the sill, and, pushing the panel so that it opened properly, thrust her body after it, falling through the alcove and onto the small landing, which brought the entire curtain down on top of her. She struggled out of it, and leaned back through the alcove, pulling the window shut and hammering its bolt into place with her fist.

Gasping for breath, she retreated up onto the top landing. But only then did she notice that the entire house was now in darkness. She gazed around, helpless. As her eyes attuned, she saw again those black apertures denoting bedroom doorways; she focused on Miriam's. Someone was standing there. Berni tried to cry out, but it was too late. Miriam came across the landing with a screech. Above her head, glittering in the moonlight, Berni saw the steel of the sewing shears. She threw herself aside, but the blades still ploughed down the back of her right shoulder, inflicting a burning wound.

Berni gasped as she tottered away.

"You dare invade my home?" Miriam hissed, her moonlit features crazed beyond recognition, streaked with sweat-soaked hair. "You hooligans dare come in here, after everything you've already done!"

She slashed with the shears again. Berni, still off-balance, crashed hard against the banister and, unable to help herself, twisted and toppled over it. Her breath caught in her throat as she cartwheeled downwards, but somehow her left hand caught the banister rail and clung to it for dear life. Agonised, she swung over the abyss by one hand.

"Miriam …" she stammered. "Miriam, it's me."

The banister groaned as if ready to buckle. She tried to find purchase with her other hand, but the mangled shoulder prevented her lifting her arm even an inch.

"I know who it is," Miriam tittered, her jack-o-lantern face appearing overhead. "But you are as much one of them as Kenyatta himself. You've *always* been a trespasser in our lives."

Berni felt cold steel as the sewing shears were inserted around the little finger of her left hand. "For God's sake, Miriam! If *you're* the one responsible for these crimes …"

"You know who's responsible. But you've locked him out. Therefore I must take his place."

"Miriam, no …"

SNIP!

Berni screamed as white fire lanced down her arm, but still she hung on.

When the shears clamped around her second finger, her anguish turned to rage. The blades sliced home again, and she fell, but not without lunging through the spindles, catching hold of those voluminous skirts. Miriam squawked as she was dragged against the flimsy banister, which sagged beneath their combined weight, and with an explosive *CRACK*, gave way.

They dropped for an eternity. At the bottom, Berni hit the stair-rail with her back; it was a brutal blow, which seemed to knock the very life out of her, though even as she somersaulted away from it and caromed against the wall, she saw Miriam land head-first on the stair itself.

The next thing Berni knew, the carpet was resting against her cheek and there was a thunderous knocking on the front door.

"Police!" a voice boomed. "We've had a report someone was seen entering through an upstairs window. Open up, or we'll force our way in!"

Splinters erupted as some heavy object was weighed against the door. Dank air and cold moonlight plumed through as burly shapes filled the hall. Electric torch beams swept back and forth, before someone hit the main light-switch. The glare half-blinded Berni, but soon a male voice was speaking gently into her ear, and a foil blanket being laid across her. The last thing she remembered before drifting out of consciousness was seeing Miriam's bloodstained hand hanging limp between the spindles on the staircase.

Berni's dreams were no respite. She was climbing ivy again, though it stretched above her to an infinite distance. Meanwhile, something was climbing after her, something that moved with simian speed and grace …

Her eyes flirted open, and she found herself in an enclosed space, her neck fixed in a brace. A man and woman in green boiler suits were busying around her. There was a rumble of wheels; the enclosed space was juddering.

"It's okay," the woman said in a soothing tone. "Everything's going to be okay."

Berni wasn't sure how, but she had a strong suspicion that *nothing* was going to be okay. "Miriam …" she stuttered, "not …"

"Try to rest."

Berni winced as a needle punctured her arm.

She'd only been taken to *Accident & Emergency* once before, when, as a child, she'd fallen from a climbing frame. It was much the same experience now: rapid movement as she was wheeled beneath clusters of dazzling lights, lots of people around her exchanging views, but basically ignoring her when she tried to speak to them. She knew there was something she had to tell them, but she couldn't think what it was.

"Not … Miriam …" she murmured.

"Relax, Bernadette," someone said. "You're going to be

fine."

She was lifted onto a bed, and they drew curtains around her. Here they removed her clothes and probed the lower parts of her body, particularly her legs.

"Can you feel anything, Bernadette?"

"Miriam …" she mumbled. "Not …"

When something sharp pressed into the sole of her foot, she reacted, her leg jerking.

"Good," someone said.

"Alone …" Despite her grogginess, Berni felt increasingly panicked, and now she was beginning to remember why. "Miriam … not …"

"Don't worry about Miriam. It's *you* we need to concentrate on."

Another needle was applied to her arm, and darkness swirled in, blotting out her vision in pieces, as though she was being buried under a deluge of leaves.

The ivy again reached up an impossible distance, but now she could see a window above. Two figures were leaning down, watching her progress. She clambered towards them, but her body was aching, in particular her back. The figures became clearer; they were Don and Miriam, and they were smiling as though to encourage her. But they didn't offer a helping hand, not even when she was close. In fact, when she was close she saw that they weren't smiling at all – they were laughing. She risked a glance downwards. Skulking darkness was rising after her. She climbed all the harder, though the ache in her back was unparalleled with anything in her prior experience. She'd almost reached the window when she saw Miriam and Don withdrawing.

She tried to scream, but no words came out.

As the window closed, she reached up despairingly – and a hand caught her arm.

It was thin, dirty, covered in coarse hair.

The nails on its fingers were black hooks.

Berni would have leapt up from where she lay, but that was

impossible given that she was bound into her bed with a framework of straps and orthopaedic supports. Her eyelids fluttered in the dim light. Somewhere to one side, a machine was bleeping. She heard footsteps, and a face appeared above her. It was pudgy and unshaved, with a mop of greasy black hair combed over the top of it.

"Hello Bernadette," the face said. "Remember *me?* I'm Detective Sergeant McAllister. I used to drive the fast-response car with your Don."

"Mir ... iam ..." she stammered. Her mouth was terribly dry, her lips cracking and sticky. "She's not ..."

"Can't tell what you're saying, love. Miriam was Don's mum, wasn't she? I don't think you should worry yourself about her at the moment."

Berni tried to shake her head, but her neck had been totally immobilised.

"You're clearly not yourself yet," McAllister added. "Understandable after all the sedatives they've shot into you. The main thing is you're going to be alright. But we'll need to talk in the morning, yeah? Whoever was seen climbing through that window attacked you savagely. You sleep now, and try to remember anything you can about him." He backtracked away across a small room. "You're in Layburn Infirmary, by the way. That's a long way from the Bannerwood. So you're perfectly safe."

Berni didn't think she could be safe anywhere now. In fact, she knew she couldn't.

"I've even got two lads out in the corridor, so nothing can happen to you. Don's on his way too. He had to find someone to cover the rest of his shift, but he'll not be long."

She could no longer form speech. Her drug-addled consciousness was ebbing away.

"That reminds me," McAllister said from the door. "I've had one of our PCs bring you some gear. I spoke to Don on the phone and he told me you had an overnight bag at your mother-in-law's. Well it's over there."

Tok

In the corner of Berni's fading vision, the pink-flowered shape of her holdall perched on an armchair. Frantic spittle frothed between her lips.

"You get some kip," McAllister said, banging the door closed behind him.

Berni put everything she could into a last effort to scream his name, but it came out a barely audible whimper. At the other side of the room, the holdall's zip was already working its way down.

LITTLE PIG

Anna Taborska

Piotr waited nervously in the International Arrivals hall of Heathrow Airport's Terminal 1. Born and bred in London, Piotr had never thought of himself as the type of guy who would import a wife from Poland. His parents had made sure that he'd learnt Polish from an early age; while his English friends had played football or watched *Swap Shop* on Saturday mornings, Piotr had been dragged kicking and screaming to Polish classes in Ealing. But it had all paid off in the end when he went to Poland one summer and met Krystyna. Since that time, Krystyna had moved to London and moved in with Piotr. They were engaged to be married, and it seemed to Piotr that all the members of Krystyna's family had already visited London and stayed with them – all, that is, except Krystyna's grandmother, and that was who Piotr was now waiting for. Krystyna had not been able to get the day off work, and Piotr was now anxiously eyeing every elderly woman who came through the arrival gate, in the hope that one of them would match the tattered photograph that Krystyna had given him.

Eventually a little old lady came out alone. Piotr recognised her immediately and started to walk towards her, stopping abruptly as he saw the woman slip, drop her glasses and, in a desperate effort to right herself, step on them, crushing them completely. Upset for the woman, Piotr began to rush forward, only to halt as she started to laugh hysterically. She muttered something under her breath and, had he not known any better, Piotr could have sworn that what she said was "little pig!"

*

The sleigh sped through the dark forest, the scant moonlight reflected by the snow lighting up the whites of the horse's eyes as it galloped along the narrow path, nostrils flaring and velvet mouth spitting foam and blood into the night. The woman cried out as the reins cut into her hands, and screamed to her children to hang on.

The three little girls clung to each other and to the sides of the sleigh, their tears freezing onto their faces as soon as they formed. The corner of the large blanket in which their mother had wrapped them for the perilous journey to their grandparents' house had come loose and was flapping violently in the icy air.

"Hold on to Vitek!" the woman screamed over her shoulder at her eldest child, her voice barely audible over the howling wind. But the girl did not need to be told; only two days away from her seventh birthday, she clung onto her baby brother, fear for her tiny sibling stronger than her own terror. The other two girls, aged two and four, huddled together, lost in an incomprehensible world of snow and fear and darkness.

The woman whipped the reins against the horse's heaving flanks, but the animal was already running on a primal fear stronger than pain. The excited yelps audible over the snowstorm left little doubt in the woman's mind: the pack was gaining on the sleigh – the hungry wolves were getting closer.

That winter had been particularly hard on the wolf pack. The invading Russian army had taken the peasants' livestock and, with no farm animals to snatch, the wolves had been limited to seeking out those rabbits and wild fowl that the desperate peasants and fleeing refugees had not killed and eaten. Driven half-mad with starvation, the wolves had already invested an irrevocable amount of energy in chasing the horse, and instinct informed them that it was too late to give up now – they had to feed or had to die.

The horse was wheezing, the blood freezing in its nostrils as it strained through the snow. Its chestnut coat was matted with sweat whipped up into a dirty foam. Steam rose off its back like smoke, giving the bizarre impression that the animal was on fire.

The woman shouted at the horse, willing it on, and brought

the reins down against its flanks. She had only been fending for herself for three days – since the soldiers had tied her husband to a tree, cut off his genitals and sawn him in half with a blunt saw – but she knew instinctively that without the horse she and her children would die. If the starving wolves did not kill them, the cold would. They still had many miles to travel – and they would never make it on foot. The time had come to resort to the last hope her children had left.

The woman pulled on the reins, slowing the horse to a more controlled pace. She tied the reins to the sleigh, the horse running steadily along the forest path. She tried not to look at her shaking, crying children, clinging onto each other as they were thrown around the sleigh – the pitiful sight would break her, and she must not break. She must not lose the battle to keep her children alive.

"Good girls," she muttered, without looking back, "hold on to your brother." She stood up carefully in the speeding sleigh and reached over the side, unfastening the buckles on the wicker basket attached there. She opened the lid as slowly and as carefully as the shaking sleigh would allow. The sight that greeted her made her stomach turn, as fear for her children gave way to shock and panic. She howled in despair. A sudden jerky movement sent her sprawling back into the sleigh. She pulled herself up and clawed at the basket again, tearing the whole thing off in an effort to change the unchangeable.

"Little pig!" screamed the woman, her eyes wild and unseeing. The children screamed too, the madness in their mother's voice destroying the last remnant of safety and order in their world. "Little pig!" she screamed. "They took the little pig!"

The woman fell back onto her seat. The horse was slowing. An expectant howl pierced the darkness behind the sleigh. The woman grabbed the reins and struck at the horse's flanks again. The animal snorted and strained onwards, but even in her panic the woman knew that if she tried to force any more speed out of it, she would kill it, and all her children with it.

Little Pig

The howling and snarling grew closer, forcing the horse's fear onto a new level. It reared and tried to bolt, almost overturning the sleigh, but its exhaustion and the snow prevented its escape from the hungry pack.

The wolves were beginning to fan out on either side of the sleigh, still behind it, but not far off. One of the beasts – a battle-scarred individual with protruding ribs and cold yellow eyes – broke away from the others and made a dash for the horse, nipping at its heels. The horse screamed and kicked out, catching the wolf across the snout and sending it tumbling into the trees. It pulled itself up in seconds and started back after its companions.

The reins almost slipped from the woman's bleeding, freezing hands. She tightened her grip, wrapping the reins around her wrists. If only they were closer to her parents' village, she could let the wolves have the horse – it was the horse that they were after. But without the horse they would all freeze in the snow long before they reached safety.

The pack was catching up with the sleigh now; the wolves spilled forward, biting at the horse. The woman shouted at the wolves, whipped at them and at the horse with the reins, but there was nothing she could do. She cast a glance at her daughters: the two little ones pale as sheets, Irena holding onto Vitek as if he were life itself. And Vitek – her perfect little boy. The woman remembered her husband's face when she first told him he had a son. His face had lit up; he had taken the little boy from her and held him in his big, strong arms … her husband … then an image of the last time she had seen him – seen his mutilated corpse tied to the old walnut tree in the orchard …

She was back in the present, fighting to save her children – losing the fight to save her children. The little pig was gone – she had put it in the wicker basket at the side of the sleigh and fastened the straps when the soldiers were getting drunk inside her house. She had gone back to the barn to get the children, to flee with them under cover of darkness to what she hoped

126

Little Pig

would be the relative safety of her parents' village. Someone must have seen her put the piglet in the basket, someone cruel enough to take the time to do up the straps after sentencing her children to death in the wolf-infested forest.

The little pig was gone and another sacrifice was needed in its place to protect the horse. The woman prepared to jump out of the sleigh. She turned to Irena and shouted, "Give Vitek to Kasia!" Irena stared at her mother blankly. "Give your brother to Kasia!" The woman's voice rose to a hysterical pitch. Four-year-old Kasia clung onto her two-year-old sister, and Irena began to cry, clutching her brother even tighter. "Give him to her!" screamed the woman, "I need you to hold the reins!" But even as she said it, she knew that the six-year-old would never be able to control the terrified horse. Her own hands were a bloody ruin and she wondered how she was able to hang on as the frantic animal fought its way forward.

"Irena! Give Vitek to Kasia – now!" But Irena saw something in her mother's eyes that scared her more than the dark and the shaking sleigh and even the wolves. She clutched her brother to her chest and shook her head, fresh tears rolling down her face and freezing to her cheeks.

A large silver wolf clamped its jaws onto the horse's left hind leg. The horse stumbled, but managed to right itself and the wolf let go, unable to keep up with the horse in the deep snow – but not for long. As the chestnut reeled, the sleigh lurched and the woman panicked. She had to act now or lose all her children. She could not give her life for them because they would never make it to safety without her. But a sacrifice had to be made. If she could not die to save her children, then one of them would have to die to save the others. She would not lose them all. One of them would have to die and she would have to choose. The delicate fabric of the woman's sanity was finally stretched to its limits and gave way. She threw back her head and howled her anguish into the night. All around her the night howled back.

The woman turned and looked into the faces of her children.

A sharp intake of breath – like that taken by one about to drown. She took the reins in one hand, and with the other she reached out for her beloved son – her husband's greatest joy; the frailest of her children, half-frozen despite his sister's efforts to keep him warm, too exhausted even to cry, and the least likely to survive the journey.

"Give him to me!" she screamed at Irena. The girl struggled with her mother. The woman wrenched her baby out of her daughter's grasp and held him to her, gazing for a moment into his eyes. The woman smiled through her tears at her son. Snow was falling on the baby's upturned face, the frost had tinged his lips a pale blue, but in the woman's fevered mind, her baby smiled back at her.

Two of the wolves had closed in on the horse and were trying to bring it down. The woman screamed and threw Vitek as far from the sleigh as she could. There was a moment's silence, then a triumphant yelping as the wolves turned their attention away from the horse, and rushed away into the night. Irena cried out, and her little sisters stared uncomprehendingly at their mother, who screamed and screamed as she grabbed the reins in both hands and whipped the horse on into the dark.

As the first light of dawn broke across the horizon, an eerie sight greeted the sleepy village. The sleigh rolled in slowly, as the exhausted horse made it within sight of the first farmhouse. It stood for a moment, head drooping, blood seeping from its nostrils, its mouth, from open wounds along its flanks. Then it dropped silently to the ground and lay still. In the sleigh sat a wild-eyed woman, staring but unseeing, her black hair streaked with white, reins clenched tightly in her bloody hands. Behind her were three little girls. Two were slumped together, asleep. The third girl, the eldest of the three, was awake – she sat very still, eyes wide, silent as her mother.

*

"Irena?" Piotr reached the old lady and touched her arm. "I'm

Piotr." He bent down and picked up what was left of Irena's glasses. "I'm sorry about your glasses," he told her, handing the crushed frames back to her.

"No need to be sorry," said Irena. "It's just a little pig."

Piotr was taken aback. It was bad enough taking care of Krystyna's relatives, but she had never said that her grandmother was senile.

Irena read Piotr like an open book.

"A little pig," she explained, "a small sacrifice to make sure nothing really terrible happens … during my visit,"

"I understand," said Piotr. He did not understand, but at least there was some method in the old lady's madness, and that was good enough for him. He paid the parking fee at the ticket machine, and they left the building: a tall young man pushing a trolley and a little old lady clutching a pair of broken glasses.

CASUALTIES OF THE SYSTEM

Tina and Tony Rath

"There is such a thing," said Mr Scroggins heavily, "as having *too* much of a good thing."

Mr Witherspoon peered at the papers Mr Scroggins had placed before him on the highly polished table. "Ah … do you think so? H'm – h'm – I suppose excess is always bad. '*Medio tutissimus ibis*,' as – er – Ovid has it."

Mr Scroggins looked at him with bulging-eyed incomprehension, and he translated, kindly, "the middle road is the safest way – moderation in all things. But is it *possible* to have an excess of good? An interesting philosophical question." He smiled hopefully.

"We are not here to discuss philosophy, Mr Witherspoon," Mr Scroggins informed him. "We are here to discuss the record of your Young Persons Rehabilitation Department."

"Ah," said Mr Witherspoon. "Well. In that case I think we had better have some coffee."

"I have ordered some, Mr Witherspoon," said Mrs Taylor. She was a soft-faced, apparently rather nervous lady, who currently represented the Probation Department. Mr Scroggins had instantly tabled her as being Not Up to the Job, which made her record all the more extraordinary. And suspect.

"Splendid, splendid," Mr Witherspoon was saying, "we can always rely on you, Mrs Taylor."

She looked as if she would be about as useful as a lace parasol in a thunderstorm thought Mr Scroggins, and then mentally amended that to a lace parasol with a long metal tip. Dangerous as well as useless. She would Break Down Under Stress. And that as far as he could see, went for the lot of them. Mr Witherspoon maundered on like an elderly classics master – from Central Casting – he wouldn't last five minutes in a real school. Mr Hornbeam must be well past retirement age, plus he seemed to be deaf, or perhaps he was just not sufficiently interested in the proceedings to listen. Mr Scroggins was an emissary from the new Department of Political Awareness, and occupied a position roughly corresponding to that of the late Witchfinder General, being employed to sniff out backsliding and failings to take cognisance of the new climate of ferocious political correctness. He was not accustomed to people who did not listen to him. The rest of the rabble sitting round the table was just that. Rabble. One of them was ACTUALLY LOOKING AT HIS WATCH.

Mr Scroggins opened his mouth to administer a magisterial rebuke. At precisely the same moment the door also opened and an unbelievably ancient woman (surely she must be past statutory retirement age as well? He must look into their retirement policies – it was amazing what appalling derelictions you found in places like this when you just lifted one stone …) came in with a trolley. No group of people can have coffee poured for them without a whole babel of "Milk?" "Sugar?" "Very weak/strong for me please," "Is there any tea?" "Could you pass the biscuits?" and even, horrifyingly, "Just touch my cup, Mabel, you'll make it sweet enough for me," from someone surely old enough to know better than to indulge in what could well be construed as sexual harassment, and the moment passed. Even Mr Scroggins realised this. He waited with barely concealed impatience until everyone was coffeed to his or her satisfaction and the awkward one provided with a cup of tea. Then he tore into the matter closest to his heart.

"You have too many successes," he announced.

Half a dozen faces turned towards him. They did not, he noticed, look at all surprised. They simply looked mildly inquiring, like cattle peering over a hedge.

"Over the past year," Mr Scroggins said, in tones of direst foreboding, "the rate of youth crime in this district has fallen," he almost said disastrously, but changed it in time to "unbelievably. Every male person remitted to your department is now either in full- or part-time education, training, or gainfully employed. Or a combination thereof. One," he frowned down at the paper he had retained, "is married *as well as* being in full-time employment, and two appear to have entered a seminary." He coughed, not sure whether these should have been counted as failures. He certainly did not consider they were either being educated *or* trained, but he decided to leave them for later, and to attack his main objective: "But there are three who seem to have vanished from your books entirely."

"Jason Doakes, Wayne Trenchard, and Hannibal Toop," murmured Mrs Taylor.

"Hannibal?" Mr Scroggins repeated incredulously.

Mrs Taylor cleared her throat nervously, "His mother was a great admirer of a cinematic production, I believe, dealing with, er …"

"Murder and cannibalism," Mr Witherspoon murmured rather apologetically.

"Yes," said Mrs Taylor, "well, with a start like that …"

Mr Witherspoon shook his head sadly. "One of our failures," he agreed.

"Yes, but what *happened* to him?" Mr Scroggins demanded. "And to the other two, Jason and Wayne?"

"Doakes and Trenchard were, I am afraid, casualties of the system," said Mr Witherspoon.

Mr Scroggins bristled. That was one of his own phrases. It meant, in his terms, simply young offenders. Not young offenders who had vanished into thin air.

"They were some of the early entry," said Mrs Taylor. "We've – learned things since then."

"And so have the little scrotes remitted to the department. Didn't care for the idea of being casualties of the system themselves," Mr Hornbeam rumbled unexpectedly. "Stories seem to have got about – somehow," he grinned, showing a set of horrendous, brown, pipe-smoker's fangs. "Did us no end of good."

"What system?" Mr Scroggins roared.

132

"Well," Mr Witherspoon and Mrs Taylor began simultaneously, then courteously waved the other to go on. This, inevitably, resulted in an awkward silence broken only by the sound of a digestive biscuit being ground between Mr Hornbeam's teeth.

"I don't care who tells me," said Mr Scroggins, now entering his quieter – and more dangerous – phase, "just so long as somebody does."

Mr Witherspoon cleared his throat. "Well, I suppose it's *our* system. Although we *are* in discussion with other authorities who are hoping to adopt it. You see, at the beginning of this year we experimented with the system of sending some of our worst cases on – er ..." he hesitated.

"Safari," Mrs Taylor supplied.

"Precisely. On safari. To – er – find themselves. And it has been successful beyond our wildest dreams."

Mr Scroggins's eyes narrowed. It was the last thing he had expected from this backward looking, conservative mob, and he did not believe it for a moment.

"You've been sending these unfortunate lads on foreign holidays?" he said.

"Not quite holidays," Mr Hornbeam said robustly. "I'd call it work experience myself."

Everyone at the table nodded gently. "It was at your suggestion," Mrs Taylor reminded him gently.

"And you managed to *lose* three of them?"

"Not – *lose* – precisely," said Mr Witherspoon. "We do know exactly what happened to them."

"Look, you can't go pushing these lads out of your district to clutter up other peoples' lists. We could all do that and it wouldn't help."

"We didn't," Mrs Taylor protested. "Hannibal Toop *wanted* to stay."

"One of our failures," Mr Witherspoon repeated sadly.

"Refused to come back," Mr Hornbeam bellowed unexpectedly. "Got himself a job. Well, good luck him I say.

And he'll need it. Don't suppose Mr Wilde will put up with him for long."

"So he took a job with a Mr Wilde. I hope this Wilde character went through the proper checks," Mr Scroggins said. "Where is his business?"

"Lewknors Lane, off Drury Lane," said Mr Hornbeam promptly. "At Jonathan Wilde's Lost Property Office. Ugly customer, Wilde. But then, so was Toop." He cackled. "And good luck to *you* if you want to check on Wilde's suitability to – er – mentor young people. What did he call that six-year-old boy that was tried at the Old Bailey for stealing an oyster woman's rings 'A young game cock of my own breeding?' He carried him out of the court on his shoulder when the judge acquitted him out of pity. Don't see him doing that with Toop. More likely to collect the forty-pound hanging fee on him."

Mr Scroggins ignored these senile maunderings, and jotted down the address. "But if he's working in London at a known address then he must appear in your records. And if, by some unpardonable carelessness he does not, a phone call should find him."

"You won't find Wilde in any telephone directory. He lived in *eighteenth* century London," said Mr Hornbeam. "He finished on the gallows of course. With any luck so will – or has – Toop."

Mr Scroggins opened his mouth but no sound emerged.

"Now Doakes was an arsonist," said Mr Witherspoon, "he set fire to his school, amongst other buildings."

Mrs Taylor dabbed her eyes. "The school-keeper."

"The school-keeper went back for his cat. Saved it too, but he'd inhaled too much smoke. Died in hospital."

"I took poor Ginger in," Mrs Taylor said. "Of course he misses Harry, but he really has settled down very well. Such a *brave* old boy ..."

"What happened to Jason?" Mr Scroggins asked, through gritted teeth.

"His mother, as they so often do," said Mr Witherspoon,

134

"said he was no angel, but he wasn't a bad boy, really. He got blamed for things he hadn't done, she said, and he was easily led. He'd set fire to the school because he was bored. He was only really interested in dinosaurs."

"So we sent him where he'd find plenty of dinosaurs. But I rather think they found him first," said Mr Hornbeam. He slid a folder in front of Mr Scroggins. It contained some colour photographs. The keynote colour was red. They were either astonishing examples of special effects ... or they were not.

"And Wayne Trenchard?" Mr Scroggins croaked, looking away quickly.

"Trenchard mugged old ladies," Mr Witherspoon said, "you don't make huge amounts of money from that, of course. A purse with a few pounds. Perhaps a ring, almost worthless except as a treasured memento of a dead husband ... but of course old ladies don't on the whole fight back. And if they do ... well, there *were* two deaths. But it was probably fear and shock rather than actual injury, and very hard to bring home to the perpetrator ... and his surviving victims were often too frightened and confused to identify him."

"Sent *him* back to the Vikings," said Mr Hornbeam, with senile relish, "lasted three days. Someone hit *him* on the head. Good riddance."

"And then, of course, word got round," said Mr Witherspoon. "Offences, as you have noticed, began to drop quite dramatically. If you know you risk spending even just a few weeks as a powder monkey on *The Victory*, for instance, or a drummer boy at Waterloo or even just in a Marylebone workhouse in the eighteen-fifties – well a lot of crime probably doesn't seem worth while. It's even worthwhile staying sober if you know you can't control yourself when you're drunk – or at least staying at home."

"And for the milder cases there's always nineteenth century Eton," said Mr Hornbeam. "They think it's a soft option. But they learn ..." he cackled reminiscently. "Terrible food. Ghastly accommodation. Greek. Latin. Swishings ... and I believe it was worse back then."

"Or they can take a course in pyramid building. Healthy outdoor life, plenty of exercise, splendid diet consisting mainly of lentils with lots of garlic and onions …" Mr Witherspoon offered.

"*And* those overseers with whips," said Mr Hornbeam, jovially, "still you only have to *mention* the Black Death to have them blubbing and begging for the pyramids. Although I have a theory that we're all descendants of the ones who *survived* the Black Death, so we've probably got natural immunity, but no one yet's had the guts to give it a try. Even when I offered an incentive of half a crown and a week off their sentence," he added in an aggrieved tone. "No backbone, lads, these days. No sense of adventure."

"So," said Mr Scroggins in the tones of one humouring several possibly dangerous loonies. "You send your young offenders back in time."

They nodded.

"And how do you do that?"

"Witchcraft, dear," said a voice from the end of the table. He realised that the lady with the trolley had remained for their discussion. She was sitting down, leaning her elbows on the table in a way Mr Scroggins found unnecessarily familiar. "The further back you go the easier it is. Can't do the twentieth century at all, which I suppose is a good thing. Can't have people going back and interfering with the time lines. Anything earlier and any changes you make seem to iron themselves out – over the years."

Mr Witherspoon nodded. "We are very lucky to have, in Mabel, a most proficient psychic practitioner – I think Mr Scroggins would prefer that term to 'witch', Mabel – who has discovered not only how to manipulate the time portals with remarkable precision, but how to set up surveillance cameras so that we can keep on eye on our clients' progress. And record it, of course."

He passed Mr Scroggins a whole pile of folders. He leafed

through them. The photographs were beautifully crisp and clear (they had been rather too clear in the case of Jason Doakes – those prints left no doubt at all about his fate). Of course they were stills from films. He could have them identified without any difficulty – and pictures of the youthful clients of the Rehabilitation Department had simply been Photoshopped into them (although how they had managed it with the – the *fragments* of Jason Doakes he could not think). He was quite sure that everyone in the room was either quite mad, or indulging in a very silly and elaborate hoax. The department would be closed. There would be sackings – there would be … a detail occurred to him which would destroy the whole silly tissue of lies at once.

"Your rehabilitation centre is always full. Where do the – er – residents come from?"

"We have a reciprocal programme," Mrs Taylor said

"We do indeed," said Mr Hornbeam. "Get an intake of work'us boys, feed them up, teach them about the rights of man – and woman – and you'd be amazed how they jolly things up for the authorities when they go back."

"But how," Mr Scroggins inquired cunningly, "do you persuade them to go *back*?"

"Most people want to go home, however bad that home may be. Some have mothers whom they discover that they love, sometimes much more than they realised, many have friends and families – and sweethearts," said Mrs Taylor gently. "Hannibal Toop was quite a surprise. Perhaps he had no one."

"*That* wouldn't be a surprise," Mr Hornbeam muttered.

"We have kept a few. Mrs Taylor, for instance, has adopted two little refugees from the Thirty Years War," Mr Witherspoon said.

"Hansel and Gretel," Mrs Taylor agreed, "we really," (her voice broke a little) "really couldn't send them back. They had seen things you could not *believe*. Except of course we know that they were true. Are true. I have had to become vegetarian. Little Gretel cannot *endure* the smell of cooking meat …"

137

Mr Scroggins glared round. "Hansel and Gretel is about right," he snarled. "Because I think you lot have been telling me a lot of fairy tales."

"Their names are not really Hansel and Gretel," Mrs Taylor said, with a sudden accession of quiet dignity. "They couldn't tell us what their real names were. The little boy has only just started to speak. The little girl gave me two German words that could be roughly translated as Chops and Steak. I think they may have been called this as a – a – joke – on the part of the … of whoever had been holding them prisoner."

"There is a surprising amount of truth hidden in fairy stories," said Mr Hornbeam, with sudden gravity. "Think – but not too hard – about why a child could have been frightened so badly by a simple kitchen smell. She and the boy, by the way, were being kept in a kind of chicken coop. They could barely move, and they were filthy … but they were being well fed," he paused, then added, "one of our lads found them and got them out. We brought the lot of them back, remitted the rest of his sentence and found him a job. Deserved it."

"Supposing – just supposing – I were to believe this farrago of nonsense," said Mr Scroggins, trying not to think of any such thing, "how do you justify your treatment of these unfortunate children?" He thumped his palm on the photographs to make it clear which unfortunates he was talking about.

Mr Witherspoon rose up. "But they were not children. Doakes, Trenchard and Toop were, by any standards except yours, young men. The State itself concedes that they were old enough to marry. My grandfather was serving his country at their age. Trenchard was taller than I am and certainly a good deal stronger. He was capable of work but he chose to make his money by robbing the most vulnerable people in our society, women, elderly and frail *women* – like our mothers and our grandmothers, who are entitled to our help and protection – to our *respect* – by any standards. We sent him to a society where he could have thriven but he chose, instead, to continue his attacks upon the old and frail. And he paid the price. Doakes was quite sane, but he was ridden with hatred, hatred for the school which tried to teach and control him, for the homes he did not own – reckless of human life, he killed a better man than he would ever have become to feed his mindless appetite for destruction ... and he finally fed an appetite greater although more innocent than his own. And Toop – Toop has found his master in Wilde, thief and thief-taker, a murderer who used the law to carry out his murders for him, and who died at last by his own instrument of murder, the hangman's rope."

But Mr Scroggins could bear no more. He stood up. "Very well. Very well, Mr Witherspoon," he said, "you will be hearing from me shortly."

He strode to the door.

"No, dear," said Mabel, "this way."

She had opened another door, a door in the blank wall. A door that was not could not be there. Beyond it was darkness and a hot swampy smell. And he could hear things out there – huge things lumbering through the dark. Mr Hornbeam, showing a surprising turn of speed, tipped him through the opening before he had even thought of taking evasive action.

And it closed behind him.

HOW THE OTHER HALF DIES

John Llewellyn Probert

"Happy, darling?"

Duncan Drysdale glanced at his wife and dropped the gleaming Daimler down a gear as the car approached their country home. The headlights gleamed off the wrought iron gates, and Duncan punched in the key code to allow them access as Rachel appeared to be pondering the question before she finally gave him a reassuring smile and said,

"Of course I am, darling. Very happy."

The glossy black barrier began to open towards them. Duncan looked at his wife. He still found her astonishingly pretty, even after ten years of marriage. He reached across and took her hand.

"And you promise you weren't too upset by the conversation this evening?"

She shook her head.

"Not really," she said. "But I have to admit I wasn't expecting that kind of subject matter to be discussed over food."

Duncan eased off the handbrake as the car began the slow mile-long journey up to the house. He had kept meaning to get lights installed, but it was yet another thing he hadn't managed to get around to ordering someone else to sort out. As the gates swung noiselessly shut behind them he realised he still felt a little guilty for mixing business with pleasure this evening.

"I know," he said, "and believe me I'm truly sorry. I hadn't realised that Martin had wanted to go over things, or that there was such urgency about the matter." He reached across and squeezed her thigh. "Thanks for being so wonderful about it all."

"Oh, I was all right." Under his hand he felt her shiver despite the confident tone of her voice. "I suppose I just still find it hard to believe sometimes that there are people in this

140

world who are capable of doing such ... terrible things."

"Well there are a few less now thanks to Martin and his team," Duncan replied, squinting into the darkness ahead of him. "And with everything pretty much resolved all that's left for me to do is make sure the general public knows all about it."

There was a nervous giggle from beside him. "I can't believe he gave you all that stuff this evening as well," Rachel said. "All the equipment he said they used."

"Well I can understand him not wanting to hang onto any of it any longer than necessary," said Duncan. "After all he found the entire business extremely distasteful. And it will all help to add weight to my report."

"But some of the things you've got in the boot!" Rachel sounded shocked now, but did he detect just the tiniest hint of a thrill as well? "A lot of the stuff might be considered obscene, but I have to admit some of the things did made me smile."

"Really?" Duncan found that hard to believe. "Like what?"

There was a rattle as Rachel held something up.

"Like these, for instance."

Duncan glanced from the road to the silhouette of his wife and back again. In the brief moment in which he looked at her he was able to make out twin hoops of what was most likely metal and he realised instantly what they were.

"When did you manage to get hold of the handcuffs?" he said, trying to keep the grin out of his voice.

"When he handed you the bag and you swung it into the boot I saw them poking out and just fancied seeing what they were like," came the innocent-sounding reply. "And then you never gave me a chance to surreptitiously put them back."

"Yes, well," he said, doing his best to sound admonishing, "those handcuffs are evidence that I'll be using, along with everything else that's in there, so make sure you put them back in the bag as soon as we get up to the house."

"Straight back?" was the teasing reply.

"Straight back," Duncan said, nowhere near as firmly as he knew he should have.

Haverford Manor had stood surrounded by woodland since the mid-1800s. The Drysdales had bought it a couple of years ago, after Duncan had ascended to the higher echelons of his chosen profession. It was a decent sized country house whose ivy-covered exterior by day exuded rustic charm, but by night resembled a ragged slumbering beast that blocked out the starlight. Once Duncan had put some of the lights on, Rachel helped him carry the bag inside. They left it just inside the front door, its contents clanking metallically as they put it down.

"I'm not sure if I like having their stuff in our house," Rachel said, wrinkling her very attractive nose.

"It's just for tonight," said Duncan. "I'll take the whole lot with me when I leave tomorrow."

"Oh, God, yes, tomorrow," said Rachel kicking off her shoes. "I wish they'd give you a bit more time to recover before getting you to start work again." Duncan followed her through into the drawing room, keeping the lights dim and fixing them both gin and tonics from a drinks cabinet in the shape of a globe as Rachel threw herself down on a divan upholstered in magenta velvet. "I mean like you said," she continued after a sip of Hendricks, "the case has already been through a court of law. Those awful people aren't going to be making any more of their dreadful films so what's the rush?"

Duncan sat opposite her in his favourite oxblood wingback leather armchair and put his feet on a stool that had been supporting Lords of the Manor for over a hundred years. Not surprisingly it creaked a little as he did so. "Because, my darling," he said as he nursed his drink, "despite the fact that the individuals concerned have been arrested, tried and convicted, the practice of making films in which individuals are tortured purely for the purpose of making money and, one presumes, the sexual gratification of certain twisted individuals, is still ongoing all over the world and I and those

142

who agree with me propose to bring a stop to as much of what we so politely refer to 'inappropriate behaviour' as is humanly possible." He took a deep swig from his glass, relishing the sensation of the alcohol as it caressed his throat with the sweetest of fire. "And the public in general are far more likely to be persuaded to read about such atrocities if they can see some of the equipment that's actually used."

"But some of those things!" Rachel tucked her feet beneath her and frowned. "Those straps, they looked so … so … uncomfortable. And as for some of those metal things – the clamps and the knives and those weird instruments with all those prongs sticking out of them …"

She looked up suddenly as if startled, then shivered again.

"Are you cold?" Duncan asked. Rachel shook her head and raised her hand for silence. The two of them sat there in the quiet of the evening as Rachel strained as if listening for something.

There it was again. A noise from above them. A creaking footstep on the only part of the upstairs that wasn't carpeted.

"That's what I thought I heard before," Rachel whispered. "Someone's on the landing."

Duncan raised a finger to his lips, got to his feet, and put down his drink. It could be one of the servants, but they should have left hours ago. With Rachel behind him he made his way to the door of the drawing room and eased it open a crack.

The youth who was now creeping down the broad staircase couldn't have been more than fifteen, although it was difficult to tell with the hood of his dark blue fleece pulled so tightly around his face. His right hand gripped the darkly varnished banister. In the left was the painting that hung above their bed.

"The little shit!" Duncan breathed, yanking open the door and taking the steps two at a time.

The boy barely had time to turn as Duncan brought his full weight crashing down upon him. The older man wrenched the work of art free from the burglar's grasp and handed it to Rachel before pinning the young man's arms behind him

143

amidst a torrent of abuse.

"If you don't shut up I'll make you," Duncan growled, holding the boy's scrawny wrists behind his back in a single meaty fist. As the curses faded quickly to whimpers and then silence, Duncan turned to Rachel.

"Is it damaged?" he said.

Rachel nodded.

"He's scratched the frame," she said, her initial shock overcome and anger beginning to appear in her eyes. "The little bastard," she added.

"Yes, and who knows what else he's damaged upstairs or already taken while we were out," said Duncan. Increased pressure on the burglar's already taut wrists elicited a yelp of pain. "Never mind that. What's your name, son?"

"Fuck off," came the reply, muffled by the thick pile of the carpet the lad's face was currently pressed into. Duncan turned back to Rachel.

"This is useless," he said. "Call the police." At the magic word the youth began to struggle again. Shifting the pinned wrists to his left hand, Duncan balled his right into a fist and delivered a deafening blow to the right side of the boy's head. "And you behave yourself, sonny, or there'll be more where that came from."

"They want to know if anyone's been hurt," said Rachel, clutching the mobile she'd made the call from.

Duncan looked at the blood trickling from the boy's ear.

"Tell them not yet," he said, his voice filled with menace.

"They also want to know how many of them there are."

Duncan paused. He hadn't thought of that. He gripped the boy's scalp and forced it back so he could hear what the little thief was trying to mumble.

"My mates … all upstairs … they'll fuck you over … let me go … fucker."

Duncan pressed the cursing lips back against the carpet and listened.

Silence.

"Tell the police he's on his own," he said. "Either his mates have scarpered or he thought he could lift a few things by himself."

Rachel spoke into the phone again, frowned, listened a little longer, and then rang off. She gave Duncan a resigned look.

"They said they'll be at least an hour, probably longer," she said.

"What!" Duncan exclaimed as his wife did her best to look apologetic. "Did you tell them I was restraining the assailant as you were speaking?"

"Yes, I did."

"And what did they say?"

"They said to remind you that you weren't to use undue force as you might be liable to a fine or imprisonment yourself if he was able to demonstrate evidence of any injury received at your hands."

Duncan wiped his right palm on the carpet. Fortunately it was red so the blood didn't show.

"What the hell am I supposed to do, then?" he said.

"You're supposed to let me go, mate," said a voice from beneath him. "Let me go and I might not consider pressing charges."

Duncan slapped him again.

"Oh no you don't, little shit," he said. "You're staying right here. If the police can't teach you a lesson, I'm sure I can think of something."

"Well you can't just sit on him until they come," said Rachel.

Duncan pondered. "I could, but then I suppose it would be obvious that I'd assaulted him after I'd pinned him down."

He snapped his fingers as an idea seemed to dawn.

"My darling," he said. "Have you by any chance still got those items that you showed me in the car? The ones that are used for restraining errant individuals?"

The handcuffs were by the door, next to the bag. Rachel was back with them in a flash and Duncan had them on the burglar

145

so smoothly he might have been using them all his life.

"Is there any rope in that bag?" There was. "After all," said Duncan once Rachel had procured that for him as well, "we don't want our new friend running away, do we?"

With wrists and ankles soundly secured, the youth was turned on his back. He drew in a deep breath, presumably to spit, but he was deterred by the ball gag Duncan had found in the bag and was now brandishing.

"Any naughty behaviour and you get this, do you understand?" he said.

The youth gave a meek nod.

"Good. Now, what's your name, son?"

An increasingly worried-sounding voice replied,

"Kenny."

Duncan tapped his chin as Rachel brought the bag over to them. "Kenny. Hmm. I wonder if that's your real name or if it just popped into your head on the spur of the moment. Not that it really matters – at least now we have something to call you."

"What shall we do with Kenny, darling?" Rachel regarded the wide-eyed but still defiant youngster trussed up on the stairs. "While we're waiting for the police, I mean."

"I'd better keep an eye on him here, just in case he's double jointed or one of those other funny things," Duncan replied. He appeared to give the matter some thought, and then said. "While I'm doing that why don't you check upstairs just in case he's done any other damage?"

Rachel was climbing the steps in a second, giving every sign of being glad to have a chance to get away from their prisoner. Once she was out of earshot Duncan leaned low and whispered in Kenny's ear.

"I sincerely hope for your sake that she doesn't find anything," he said to the squirming form beneath him, "because if she does, never mind what the police think, I'm going to make sure you regret coming here."

Rachel was ten minutes but it felt like longer. When she eventually made her way back down, her face was grim and there was the glint of tears in her eyes.

"Is everything all right?" Duncan called up to her.

Rachel shook her head and released a tiny sob.

"The spare room's in a mess, and so is your study," she said. "There are books all over the floor."

Duncan glowered at Kenny.

"None of them damaged I hope?" he said, not taking his eyes from the youth.

There was a pause as Rachel took a deep breath.

"Some of them have been torn from their bindings. I suppose he was looking for hidden valuables."

"Thought we might be as sneaky as he was trying to be, eh?" said Duncan, wagging a finger at his prisoner. "Naughty boy. Very naughty boy."

"I never did any of that!" blurted Kenny, lapsing back into silence after a prod from Duncan's boot.

"But that's not the worst," said Rachel, hugging her sides and trying to stop the tears. "He's gone and … gone and … on our bed oh God he's gone and …"

"HAS he?" Duncan roared at Kenny. "The mean spirited little scum."

"I never!" the boy cried again, genuine fear in his eyes now. "Look, I did stumble about a bit when I broke in, and I did look in some of the books, but I never done nothing in your bedroom. Nothing!" he gave both of them an imploring look as Duncan looked meaningfully at his wife.

"Well, we can't let someone get away with doing something like that, can we?" he said. "And somehow, despite the sterling efforts of our boys in blue to apprehend little monsters like our new friend here, I don't think the courts are going to mete out a suitable punishment for such a gross and indecent intrusion on our private life, do you?" Rachel bit her lip and nodded. "Exactly!" Duncan glared at his captive who now looked properly terrified. "What shall we do with him?"

"I think we need to take him to the playroom," said his wife, checking that the front door was locked.

"Splendid idea," said Duncan, hoisting the lad to his feet, "and exactly what I was thinking." He noticed Rachel's grimace and glanced at the front of the boy's pale blue jeans where a damp patch was spreading. "Oh dear," he said in even more menacing tones than before, "has the little boy wet himself? Has the little man lost control? Does the little man think that maybe he shouldn't have come here tonight?"

All Kenny could do was sniff away tears he was trying hard to suppress and give the two of them a weak nod.

"Well, that's a start," said Duncan. "Do you see darling – the guilty party already regrets his actions!"

"Perhaps there may be some hope for him then," Rachel said.

"Perhaps," said Duncan, gripping the boy's wrists and forcing him forward. "But I for one am not at all convinced that we have convinced him not to offend again, and we can't possibly let him go before we do."

"Of course not," said Rachel, following, "I mean we owe it to society."

"To people like ourselves."

"The ones who make society."

"Not ones who try to destroy it like our little friend here."

"Now stop struggling, Kenny," said Rachel, "or my husband will have to break one of your legs to show we mean what we say."

Kenny went limp as his stumbling, semi-protesting form was manhandled through a maze of wood panelled ground floor corridors. They passed more paintings like the one he had tried to steal, as well as framed photographs of the family, and of committees that Duncan had been proud enough to be asked to sit on. In between these were certificates and other official-looking documents that had obviously been deemed impressive enough to display. They made their way through a brightly lit kitchen and Kenny did his best not to look at the knives hanging next to the Aga, especially when Duncan paused next to them.

148

"You know, I've had an idea," Duncan said.

His wife looked at the array of sharpened steel. "Oh no, darling," she said. "Not those. After all, we cook with them."

"Oh, not those," he said with a trace of mirth. "But it just occurred to me. Could you go back and fetch the bag? The one by the front door? The one filled with you-know-what?"

While Rachel disappeared back the way they had come Duncan unlocked a side door at the back of the kitchen.

"This used to lead through to the garages," he explained, indicating the impenetrable blackness beyond. "But once we converted the stables to keep the cars we suddenly had a lot of extra space. And it's come in far more useful than we ever expected. Oh no you don't"

Despite his wrists and ankles still being bound, Kenny had hopped over to the kitchen door and was banging his head against the glass. Duncan strode over, grabbed the boy, and threw him into yawning darkness.

*

When Kenny came round he lifted his head to see the lights were on.

The teenager dragged himself to a sitting position and gazed open-mouthed at the room in which he found himself. Elegant mahogany panelling adorned every wall, as well as the raised dais ahead of him. The dais that supported the most ornately carved chair Kenny had ever seen.

In which someone was sitting.

The figure wore the wig of a high court judge, and the kind of mask the boy had seen at the circus when he was little – a grinning, unsympathetic rictus that he knew would offer him little mercy or understanding.

"Young man!"

The figure on the throne addressed him in tones Kenny realised might be Drysdale's. "Young man," it continued, "you are hereby accused of breaking and entering a property owned

149

by upstanding members of the general public, individuals who have worked hard, have paid their taxes, and who therefore feel duly obliged to some degree of protection from some of the more threatening elements of our society. You are also charged with having damaged some of their property, and also with having committed an unpardonable act upon their home. How do you plead?"

Kenny had no idea what to do, and consequently he let fly with a string of expletives.

"The time-honoured defence of the disenfranchised and the destitute!" returned the masked figure. "So be it." It looked beyond Kenny to an unseen and imagined audience. "It is therefore my solemn duty to pass sentence upon this unfortunate wastrel, this detritus of society, a society which could only benefit from the removal of such an unnecessary and harmful element." The figure looked directly at him. "I therefore sentence you to the punishment you truly deserve."

Kenny felt hands behind him, propelling him to the doorway in the far corner. He tried to dig the heels of his trainers into the polished parquet floor but it was no use. They made a terrible squeaking sound as he was manoeuvred through the doorway and into the torture chamber beyond.

For torture chamber it was. A veritable cornucopia of instruments designed for the execution of piercing, bloodletting, and for the flaying of skin. When Duncan and Rachel were finished with Kenny's prostrate form, when they had stripped his body of skin, drained it of blood and rendered it bereft of most of its muscle, the couple who had perpetrated such agonies upon their (mostly) still living victim, removed their masks, gave each other a loving look and kissed over the broken remains of the invader of their home.

"Happy, darling?" asked Duncan Drysdale.

His wife wiped the blood from where it had splashed on her face before replying. "Very happy, my darling," she said. "And so much happier than I was earlier this evening, when we had to listen to those dull little friends of yours wittering on about how they had made such 'significant inroads into improving our society'."

"I know," said Duncan, going to the sink in the corner and washing away the clumps of fat that clung to his fingers. "But it still saddens me to think that there are people out there who want to make entertainments of this kind of serious work, who even want to turn it into some kind of public sex show." He sighed. "Everything these days seems to need to be about sex, even such a serious subject as punishment."

Rachel picked up the bloodstained tawse and cleaned some of the gobbets of flesh from it. "I know," she said. "Such things really are best done in private. I'm just glad we didn't have to use our own tools for a change," she said.

Duncan grinned. "Oh I know. At least we won't have quite so much to clean this time."

Rachel looked down at the torn broken body on the table before her. "Poor little boy," she said. "But then he shouldn't have tried to break in."

"Precisely," said Duncan, picking up the camera and adjusting the focus so that Kenny's face, slashed and penetrated in the most expert fashion so that he had remained alive to experience every single punishing blow, was framed to its best advantage. "But might I be so bold as to say that pretending to telephone the police was a masterstroke?"

Rachel gave a demure little smile. "Thank you, my darling," she said. "I thought you'd appreciate that little extra touch, especially after my rather wonderful performance at being so shocked at all those terrible things I made up on the spur of the moment about what he had done to our bedroom."

"Oh, I did," replied her husband, taking shots of Kenny's ripped limbs, the muscles that he would normally have used for walking hanging limply over the sides of the table. Duncan looked up at the clock on the wall, shielded behind whatever mayhem the couple might see fit to cause in their playroom by a thick sheet of Perspex.

"We'd better get all this tidied up, and then I can add these pictures to our collection," he said, taking one last look at the remains of the young man they had systematically taken to pieces. "And then I really do need to get to bed. The stories that the upstanding members of Middle England love to read don't write themselves, you know."

"Of course darling," said Rachel, blowing Duncan a bloodstained kiss across Kenny's defiled corpse. "After all, we can't have the editor of one of Britain's most popular tabloid newspapers tired for his meeting tomorrow morning, now can we?"

MUSIC IN THE BONE

Marion Pitman

"Now your cage shall be made of the finest beaten gold
And the doors of the best ivory."
The ballad finished, the woman sat down, and a man with a
guitar stepped to the front of the room. Lena tried to stop
fidgeting. Already she had pulled a thread in her skirt on a
splinter from the table leg, and her restless fingers had
encountered a mass of old chewing gum on the underside of
the tabletop.

She took a tissue out of her bag, spat, and wiped her fingers;
she looked at her hands. They appeared grotesque and
unnatural, like alien claws. She wondered if the stigmata were
coming back; she caught a whiff of some foetid smell. Quickly
she threw the tissue in the ashtray and put her hands in her
pockets.

Tom glanced at her, frowning. He was actually listening to
this maundering sub-70s stream-of-consciousness lyric. One of
the guitar strings was slightly flat, just enough to be painful.

The room was small, smoky and cold, with mismatched
chairs, benches with holes in the red leatherette upholstery,
revealing gross intestines of grey foam, and not enough people.
Not surprising with this going on.

Her hands seemed to be wandering again, fiddling with the
silver bird-skulls in her earlobes; she missed the intro to the
next performer.

She hadn't seen him before. He started to play the fiddle.

His bow stroked and caressed the strings, producing sounds
Lena had never heard from a violin. It purred, moaned, sighed;
he made love to it, almost you heard the instrument reach
orgasm.

When he finished, the audience was silent for a moment;
then they applauded wildly.

Lena was entranced. She had never heard an instrument sing

153

so, heard music with such life and intensity.

His second number was a reel – quick, lively, vigorous; images whirled in her head, wild dancing, lightning flashes, crashing surf and waterfalls; jungles of bright birds and vivid flowers.

When it ended she felt quite breathless, and joined in the applause with abandon.

He was cute, too. Tall, thin and wiry, black hair in long tangled curls, very white skin. Small silver rings glinted in his ears. He looked glamorous, in the magical sense; dangerous; feral. Probably, she thought, he would turn out to be a computer programmer for an insurance company, with no conversation beyond Windows and war-gaming. Still, he was a good deal more decorative than Tom. She glanced sideways at Tom's bald spot, the hair around it rough and in need of a trim. Not to mention a comb.

She generally went home with Tom after the folk club. That was as far as the relationship went, spending the night together once a week. It had been going on like that for months. She felt she couldn't bear it a moment longer. She would tell Tom she had a blinding headache, or the curse had come on early.

At one time she would have chatted up the fiddle player, tried to take him home with her, just for the hell of it; but that was in another life.

The club always finished by half past ten so that the organisers could get back to some far-flung outpost of suburbia; naturally most people drifted down to the still-open bar. Lena drifted with the rest; Tom was deep in discussion with a frowning woman in a long skirt; Lena caught the words "CD drive" and "mother board". She made an impatient move away from them, and found herself next to the fiddle player.

He caught her eye and smiled.

She said, "I was very impressed by your playing. You're amazingly good," and thought, how naff does that sound?

But he looked pleased, and said, "Thank you."

She said tentatively, "I haven't seen you here before?"

"No. I only moved here recently."

"Oh, right." Pause. "Where were you before?"

"Oh, I've been living abroad."

"Uh huh?"

"Travelling."

"Right."

"Would you like a drink?"

"Oh! I'm sorry – I wasn't …"

"That's okay. But would you like a drink?"

"Thanks. I'll have a pint of Guinness."

He turned away to catch the eye of one of the young New Zealanders behind the bar.

Lena glanced round. The bar was noisy, with the jukebox on, and a lot of girls in tight jeans and skimpy tops, drinking vodka, or lurid cocktails, and having a good time at the tops of their voices. It seemed to be somebody's hen night.

She remembered a bar in – Dublin? Auckland? Cape Town? – some time in another life – a live band playing very loud, dancing all night, spaced out on too much white wine and no food, heavily snogging an extravagantly underdressed woman with red hair and big tits. She could remember the rum and coke taste of the redhead's mouth … nothing came of it. One of them had made a misstep, or they just hadn't wanted it enough. Where was she staying? a hostel, a five star hotel? – it was all the same in those days. Another life. With the Latvian footballer in Sydney, looking for a bad time in King's Cross at four a.m. … Christmas Eve in a sports bar in Wellington, high as a kite on fear and adrenaline – another life.

The fiddle player turned with the Guinness; he smiled; his teeth were flat across the front, with long canines – not Dracula-long, just slightly wolfish. His eyes were a clear dark brown, like glasses of neat whiskey.

As she took the drink from him, she noticed his hands, pale and very thin, just skin strung over bones; she touched the back of his fingers, they were smooth, like alabaster, and nearly as cold.

155

"Thanks," she said with a smile, and looked into his eyes just a little too long.

They stood together in silence for a while; he drank beer; no one spoke to them. Then Tom called,

"Lena! You coming?"

She turned. Now or never.

"Sorry," she said. "I've got a really early start tomorrow."

"Okay. See you next week," and he was gone. Just like that.

Behind her, she heard a low, teasing voice, "Have you really got an early start?"

She turned back; he was looking at her with a smile twisting up one side of his mouth.

"Maybe," she said. "Maybe not."

"My name's Ed," he said.

"Lena."

"I only live round the corner. It's very near the tube station."

"That's handy."

"Are you coming home with me?"

She stared at him. She no longer expected that sort of directness. He laughed. There seemed no reason not to say, "Yes."

*

His flat was up three flights of stairs, an attic room with a sloping ceiling, and a low window that looked out on other roofs – all angles, different heights, red, brown, grey, black, tile, slate, concrete. Street lighting gave them an eerie glow.

The room was dimly lit, the walls hung with swags of black and dark red cloth. A tall ebony and ormolu cabinet stood against one wall, on top of it a phrenology head, a malachite obelisk, a crystal ball on a blackwood stand, and one of those globes full of lightning that follows your hand. No stuffed crocodile, she thought; every alchemist's laboratory should have a stuffed crocodile.

Another wall was lined with instruments and sound

equipment; against a third was a wide divan with a black silk spread.

Ed said, "What do you think?"

"Very Gothic," she replied; "You don't look Goth."

"Oh, you should see me at weekends." He laughed.

She looked along the wall; "You play a lot of instruments."

"Fiddle and guitar mainly. Keyboards now and then. I'm trying to learn the harp."

It was a small, portable, medieval style harp, fancifully carved with wolves and unicorns.

"But the fiddle's my true love," he said. He put the case down on the bed and opened it, taking the cloth from the instrument and stroking its neck affectionately.

It was a beautiful looking thing; the wood glowed with the patina of age and loving attention; the pegs, fingerboard and bridge were inlaid with ivory or bone, a warm yellowish white. The strings, and the hair of the bow, seemed to catch the light with a golden glint. She fancied it almost hummed softly to itself, there in the case.

"You're amazingly good," she said. "I've never heard anyone play the fiddle like that."

He grinned. "So you didn't say that just as a chat-up line?"

"Actually, no. I mean, yes, all right, it *was* a chat-up line, but it was true too."

He smiled again, slowly, suggestively; left the fiddle and moved towards her. He put his hands on her hips, lowered his head, and kissed her.

She gripped his elbows to steady herself; the kiss was long and deep, hungry, demanding. He tasted of beer and cigarettes. She found her whole body responding; her belly went on fire and yearned toward him ...

At last he broke contact, and stepped back.

"D'you want a shower?" he said.

"Uh – no. I had one before I came out." She responded automatically, then thought, that was wrong.

He said, "Okay. I will, though." He kissed her lightly on the

157

forehead, and went out through a curtained doorway in the corner.

Lena wandered around. She was shy of touching anything, but she looked avidly. On a battered map-chest beside the cabinet were a laptop and some papers; beside the instruments was a tall blackwood rack with several dozen CDs, many of artists she'd never heard of, besides Steeleye Span, Pink Floyd, Nick Drake, Counting Crows, Fields of the Nephilim. Eclectic, she thought. There was Bach, too, and Sibelius, and traditional Irish fiddle players. There seemed to be several by a band called Procne.

When Ed came out she said, "Actually I think I might have a shower, if that's okay?"

"Sure," he replied. "Plenty of hot water."

She showered quickly, trying to keep her hair dry, leaving her earrings in. Her heart beat too fast, her stomach fluttered, nervous as a schoolgirl on a first date. She laughed at herself.

She came back to the bed-sitting room wrapped in a towel. Ed was naked, sitting back on the divan; he pressed a remote control, and music filled the room.

It was a fiddle, backed by keyboard and a flute or whistle. It sounded like Ed's playing.

She sat on the edge of the bed; she said, "Is that you?"

"That's Procne," he replied, "which is me."

"Just you?"

"Just me."

"Is that a flute?"

He got up and stepped across to the instrument wall, and opened a small case; he took something out and came back. He handed her a short cylinder, smooth and dull white. It was pierced like a tin whistle, but the shape was rough and irregular.

"It's a thighbone," he said.

"A human one?"

"Of course not." He was smiling; she wasn't sure whether to believe him.

158

"It's a native artefact," he said, "it makes an incredible sound." He put it to his mouth and blew softly; the notes that came out were beautiful, pure, eerie, chilling. Lena felt the hairs on her arms bristle; there was darkness in the sound, and the warning of a deadly snake unseen among leaves …

He stopped playing, and saw her expression.

"Don't you think it's wonderful?" he asked.

"Yes. But scary."

He looked at her, his head on one side; then he put the flute away, backtracked on the CD, and unwound the towel.

His response to her nakedness was immediate, and her own body also responded at once; she wanted him instantly, urgently.

The music intensified the mood; it throbbed and wailed with aching sexual need, with pounding blood.

He laid her on the divan; his caresses became rough; he bit her breasts and she cried out at the pain, but was too deep in the grip of lust to push him away.

His hands were hard, but she thrust against them, relishing the force of resistance.

Under and behind all, the music beat with the rhythm of sex, with deep lascivious notes that seemed to curl up like tongues of fire, igniting sparks all through her limbs.

But still, at the last moment, with a reflex she stiffened and pulled back, and said, "Condom."

"What?" He sounded genuinely bemused.

"Condom. I'm not on the pill. There's some in my bag if you …"

He gave a small, rather bitter laugh, and reached out to a cabinet beside the bed.

He looked at her while he put on the condom by touch; there was something in the dark eyes she couldn't quite fathom; was it just naked desire, or was there something else … ?

But she forgot it all once he began thrusting with the underlying beat of the music, which had moved on to a faster, simpler, more rhythmic track – almost, had she been able to think about it, as if he had compiled the tracks to the pace of his lovemaking.

*

Afterwards she felt not so much satisfied as drained, sucked dry. For several minutes she couldn't move.

He said, "Do you want to stay the night?"

"Uh …" She didn't really; she felt insecure, these days, sleeping away from her own place, but, "What time is it?"

"Two-thirty."

"D'you mind if I stay?" She really didn't think she had the strength of mind – or body – to go anywhere right now.

"Sure. That's okay. I'll have to throw you out early, though – I have to go to work."

"Okay."

He showered again, but Lena scarcely had the energy to stagger to the toilet. Unlike most men, Ed seemed energised by sex; he was playing something low and sinister on the flute when she fell asleep.

He woke her early, as he had said; he seemed anxious to see her go, so she showered quickly, drank the coffee he brought, left without mentioning breakfast.

As she started down the stairs, she passed a woman in a light raincoat – slim and pretty, with heavy blonde hair falling to her shoulders, who stared hard and hostilely at Lena as they passed, and Lena thought she heard a short, ironic laugh behind her.

*

When she got home, Lena went to change her clothes. She was startled and rather appalled at the number of small bruises on her arms and breasts and stomach and thighs. She didn't remember acquiring all those. She felt stiff, too, as if she had fallen, or slept on a hard floor.

160

She ran a bath; she still had over an hour before she needed to leave for the café; she wasn't on breakfasts this week.

She thought about Ed. On the whole, she thought she'd rather not see him again. The sex had been amazing; he was interesting company – and a brilliant musician, and she was always taken by people who were very good at what they did – but she didn't like feeling that far out of control.

Still, the question was unlikely to arise; in Lena's experience, men who took you to bed the first time you met seldom wanted to repeat the event.

So although he'd taken her phone number, she wasn't surprised not to hear from him. She missed the folk club the next week, and when she went the week after it was only with the faintest expectation of seeing him.

Tom had phoned three times; she had tried to put him off, but in the end she said she wanted a break from the relationship. Since Tom had never admitted that they had a relationship, he tried to argue with this; he said, "I suppose you've dropped me for that poncey fiddle player."

She said, "Don't be silly," and put the phone down.

Should she make up with Tom? She was certainly in charge of the relationship, such as it was, but he bored her so – she thought of Ed playing the thighbone flute, and was shocked at the flood of lust the thought provoked. Well, she said to herself, that would wear off.

*

Ed wasn't at the club when she arrived, and she wasn't sure if she were disappointed or relieved. But when he turned up in the interval, with the blonde from the staircase, she was definitely angry. He sketched a wave and a smile; she raised an eyebrow, said, "Hi," brusquely, and went down to the bar.

She sat there for three-quarters of an hour, drinking gin, and fantasising that he would come down alone and speak to her and explain and apologise; then she went home. The pain was

161

astonishing.

Dammit, she thought, I don't even like him. But he could have rung and warned me. Except a man wouldn't see the necessity. Not after a one-night stand. Meaning nothing. And it meant nothing to me either – God knows I'm old enough to know how these things work. She started to shake, and went to lie down. Her hands itched and smarted dreadfully.

All night she dozed and woke to the sinuous sounds of the flute and the fiddle, that seemed to have wound themselves around her brain cells. With some idea of laying the ghost, she went out on her break next day and looked in a record shop for Procne. There was nothing. She asked the assistant, but there was nothing in the catalogue. Didn't mean a thing of course; he probably just sold the CDs at gigs.

The next week she wondered whether to give the folk club a miss. Tom wasn't talking to her, and she didn't know if she could handle the humiliation of Ed's turning up with the blonde again.

In the end she went late, arriving after the interval. She slipped in during the applause; Ed was playing. He had the guitar this time. His fingers flew over the strings, as his left hand hunched and squeaked on the frets; the notes seemed sharp and glittering like shards of glass, weaving a circle, a crown of thorns, a stifling circumference of ice, dazzling in the sun. It hurt.

When he finished, the applause was deafening.

He glanced up – Lena couldn't tell if he saw her or not. She looked around, but couldn't see the blonde.

He put down the guitar and picked up the fiddle, tuned it, and began a slow air, yearning, languorous, full of hope and despair and uncertainty. Despite herself Lena found tears in her eyes.

The audience was silent for several beats after he finished, and the applause was quieter, but went on and on.

He stepped off the stage and came across to where she was standing.

"Hi," he said. "Sorry about last week."

"You could've warned me," she said, resisting the impulse to say, Oh, that's all right.

He frowned; "I suppose so."

"So is that your girlfriend? I saw her before, at your flat."

He shrugged. "She's just a friend. So are you – I hope."

She looked into his eyes and felt her stomach churning. Her mind was saying, he can't just dismiss it like that, but her body wanted him, on almost any terms.

He said, "Will you come back with me tonight?"

She found herself saying, "Yes."

*

They left early, and when they got in he poured glasses of whiskey; they sat on the divan sipping the drinks. He took the guitar out of the case, and began changing a string. The new string, out of a cloth bag with no label, glinted in the soft light of the lamps. The frets of the guitar were inlaid with strange angular patterns; he saw her looking at them, and pointed.

"Mystic runes," he said, "in an unknown language."   She raised an eyebrow, and he laughed; "It's supposed to be Arabic or something. Probably says Made in Japan."

Something rang false in his tone; she said, "All your instruments are unusual some way."

He gave a one-sided smile; "I guess I'm trying to find the perfect instrument. The guitar's good; the fiddle's better. The flute's got its own – uh – something, but it's a bit primitive. Maybe I'll find what I'm looking for with the harp."

"And what are you looking for?"

"Ah!" He gave her a big, genuine smile. "That's the sixty-four thousand dollar question. I can only say I'll know it when I find it.

"I don't know – the essence of music? The thing that all music reminds us of – the soul of music? the music of souls, perhaps?

"As you say, I, well, modify my instruments, trying to get closer to – to the heart of music, the real thing, that's more than just sound, that's being, meaning, essence … then you'd hear something."

"But how do you do it? How do you 'modify' them?"

"Ah. That, I'm afraid, is a trade secret. One day I'll tell you, I think. I think you'd understand – better than Heather."

He looked at her, and she thought, is that meant to make me feel better about Heather? but it did, all the same.

He put on another Procne CD, a gentler one this time, with a good deal of keyboard, which seemed to calm and dilute the effect of the fiddle and guitar. The flute was scarcely in evidence.

Lena took the first shower; he lent her a red silk dressing gown. While he was in the bathroom she wandered around; feeling daring, she tried the top drawer of the map chest, but it was locked. She picked up a cassette tape that lay on top behind the printer; the hand-written label said, "Edward Oliver – First Album". As she turned it to read the list of tracks, his voice, sharper than usual, said,

"Put that down!"

She dropped it and stepped back, reddening. "I'm sorry …"

"No. Sorry. I – that's a very early tape, and very bad. I'm rather sensitive about it."

He put his hands on her shoulders, and looked into her eyes, and she forgot the tape.

The sex, like the music, was slower and gentler this time, though Lena still found herself with bruises she couldn't account for. Afterwards she drifted imperceptibly into sleep.

*

They saw each other after that once or twice a week; she didn't know if he was still seeing Heather, and didn't ask. Sometimes the sex was gentle and easy; more often it was increasingly violent. Sometimes he would put his hands on her head and

164

press down and back till she was afraid her spine would snap. He was strong, and she was afraid to struggle too much. He pinched and bit her breasts, although she asked him not to. But then he would tease her until she went into orbit, making her wait for the climax, and at last igniting a pit of fire deep inside her that no one before had ever reached; and the pain would seem unimportant.

Sometimes he would play the fiddle or the guitar before they began; if he played the flute, things were more likely to get out of hand. She never heard him play the harp.

"I'm still working on it," he said.

Every time she got home, stiff and sore and black and blue, she thought, why the hell am I seeing him; but when he rang she still said Yes, and when he played she felt helpless to resist anything he wanted.

The palms of her hands stung continually; the stabbing pain in her side was back.

They didn't go out together. Once she suggested – just casually – going to a movie. His eyes veiled, and he shrugged.

"Sorry," he said, "I don't get much free time."

"Oh."

She was startled, but he quickly went on to talk about something else.

So she went home with him after the folk club, just as she had with Tom; at other times he rang quite late in the evening, when it was too late to go out anywhere, and she went to his flat. She never said, "Why don't you come over here?" – she knew he wouldn't.

Sometimes they had a take-away meal, often a bottle of wine. But most often he played music and did extraordinary, painful, amazing things to her body.

Once she stood at the window of the flat in a summer twilight, looking out at the planes and angles of the roofscape, and said, trying to sound playful,

"So what do you do in real life?"

"I work in I.T.," he said, "and it's very, very, boring, and I don't talk about it in my own time."

So she couldn't ask him any more.

*

One night, the CD was a throbbing, dark track, with an insistent beat and the flute underlying everything. The fiddle was strident, the guitar plangent; the whole pulsed with menace.

Ed was holding her head and nibbling her neck and shoulders, his hands stroking her sides, relaxing her, when suddenly she felt a pain so sharp her body jerked upright reflexively as she screamed, wrenching his hand away, her head hitting the bridge of his nose.

He yelled, "What the fuck?" as he reared back, both hands to his face, blood pouring between them.

She sat, gasping, one hand to her shoulder where his teeth had met and blood trickled down.

He threw his head back, and managed at last to stem the nosebleed. Half stunned still, she helped him clean up. Then they stood in the bathroom and looked at each other.

"What the *hell* did you do that for?" he said.

"I couldn't help it. That *hurt*."

"Are you telling me you don't like pain? You stupid bitch, you're longing for it – I can smell it, I can taste it, it comes off you in *waves*. You deafen the air with your need for pain."

"But not from *you*, you fool, not from *you*." Feet, hands and side throbbed as she spoke.

He shook his head. "Such a pity. I know I could have made it work with you. You're so strong. You don't know what you missed. I'll have to do the best I can with Heather."

She heard the words, but didn't take them in.

Suddenly, he leaned forwards, picked off with his nail the dried blood over the wound on her shoulder, blood welling up. Before she could react, he pressed a tissue to the wound, and took it back, red and wet, saying, "A souvenir."

166

All she could think of was getting away from him. She backed into the bedroom, but he made no attempt to follow. Pain hammered so hard in her palms she could scarcely get dressed.

She finally managed it, picked up her coat and bag, and hobbled out. He leaned in the bathroom doorway; but as she started down the stairs she heard him playing the flute. She forced her hands over her ears.

*

Time went by. Ed didn't call. Lena left the answering machine on; she was terrified of what would happen if she heard his voice.

She avoided the folk club. Tom started phoning again, saying he was worried about her. She told him she had a new job, working evenings.

Her boss at the café said, "I don't know what you've been on, love, but you did right to give it up."

Gradually the throbbing in her hands subsided. She thought about what Ed had said, and tried to avoid thinking about pain.

*

After about three months, a friend just back from Australia rang, and asked Lena to come to the folk club. Lena tried to put her off, but Jenny was very forceful; Lena wasn't feeling forceful.

In the end, she said, "Look, Jen, there's a chap goes there sometimes that I don't want to see. I haven't been for months."

"What, just because of some bloke? Why? What did he do?"

He bit me. No, she couldn't say that. "Well – um – we were seeing each other, and it – ended badly."

"Tom?"

"No, not Tom. Another bloke."

"Well, for God's sake, Lena, you can't run your life by

167

blokes you're avoiding. Anyway, he might be avoiding you –
you won't know if you never go."

In the end she agreed to go. At least Jenny would be some
protection.

They got there early – another of Jenny's irritating habits.
Ed was sitting on the edge of the stage, talking to Rob. Rob
knew Jenny; before Lena could protest or move, she was
dragged across the room.

Beside Ed on the stage stood the harp.

Ed said, "Hallo, Lena."

To her great relief, she didn't go into rabbit with snake
mode. Had she overestimated the power of his voice?

She said, "Hallo. Have you finally got it together with the
harp?"

He smiled; "I hope so." He stood up, and moved between
her and the instrument. "It would have been better with you."

"What? What would?"

"If you'd stayed. It would have been better. But I think I've
got it right."

He moved just a little, so she could see the harp.

She said, "You've finished customising it, then?"

"Modifying. I prefer modifying."

The wood glowed, what little one could see for the intricate,
off-white inlay, bone or ivorine, the pattern something like
Celtic knotwork, endlessly interwoven, polished and shining.
The pegs were of the same material. The strings glowed softly,
with an organic more than a metallic gold. The only thing that
marred its perfection was a small dark smear, the colour of
dried blood, on the sound-bow.

Lena found it hard to take her eyes off it. It seemed to be
mesmerising her as much as Ed had. Someone spoke to Ed;
people moved, interrupting her view of the harp, and she
managed to tear herself away, and went for a drink.

She came back after the session had started, and stood at the
back. Jenny was deep in conversation, talking over a woman
with a high, thin and barely audible voice. Lena was aware of

impatience, a feeling of marking time until Ed played the harp. After a bit she found a seat near the front, on the other side of the room from where Ed was.

He came on last before the interval, sitting down and setting up the harp on a stool. As he drew his fingers across the strings, everyone in the room fell silent, even the couple who stood at the back and had talked through every song since 1972. Lena lost all sense of time and space. She felt blinding sunlight, another time and place, and the impossible high of that week with Peter, and the intolerable pain that followed; felt as she had not allowed herself to feel since; felt again the intense joy of seeing his face, of his voice, that made her spine tingle; the smell of his skin, the smooth black skin of his shoulder, in a green singlet; he was there, he was turning towards her, smiling –

– and the music stopped, and her eyes darkened, and her body fell through fathoms –

– and she opened her eyes, and Ed was setting the harp upright on the stool, and the audience was still silent, too stunned for applause.

And then the harp sang. It sang with a woman's voice, and Ed wasn't touching it, he sat frozen, a look of utter dismay on his face. The harp sang:

"He stole my bones for ivory
  He stole my hair for gold
  He stole my blood for fire and flood
  He tried to pour away my soul
  He scoured my bones, he wove my hair,
  He poured my living blood through air
  He burned my flesh, he poured my life away
  To weave a net, a net to trap
  The music of the universe
  The sound of heaven, the sound of earth
  The music of the soul—"

It ended with a single piercing note, like a cry of intense pain –

 – and she knew. She knew what had happened to the woman on the stairs, and why she wasn't here. She knew what the harp was inlaid with – felt it, excruciatingly, in her bones. She knew what it was strung with – but surely the gold hair had been too short …

Ed was staring, his face white as bone, his eyes burning.

"I wanted it to be you," he said, "it would have been so much better with you. It should have been you …"

Lena looked away, before she read what was in his eyes. She stood, and walked out of the still silent room. In the corridor she paused. The pain in her hands was gone.

Jenny came out after her. "My God," she said, "What was that about? Lena – you all right?"

She took a deep breath; "I'm fine. Jen, I want you to come with me to a police station."

THE COAL-MAN

Thana Niveau

The long black arm snaked out of the pillow and a hand with chalky fingers closed over Jen's mouth. The fingers prised her lips open and slipped inside, crumbling to charcoal dust as they clawed their way down her throat.

Jen tore free of the nightmare with a strangled cry. She lay clutching her throat and gasping, staring into the cold darkness with wide, unseeing eyes. Her heart banged against her ribs like a caged animal. But although she strained to hear, there was no voice, no laughter, no scuttling inside the wall. Outside a breeze set the rowan creaking, but its spindly fingertips couldn't reach far enough to tap on her window.

As her eyes adjusted to the gloom, the angles of the room swam into focus. Shards of moonlight revealed the gleaming floorboards. Bare. She wanted to believe it had just been a dream. Better still a false memory. Nothing would comfort her more than knowing she was only mad. That however real it had seemed to her all those years ago, the whole thing was only the product of a disturbed child's overactive imagination. Her memories were sketchy and unreliable as it was. Why couldn't she just forget the other pieces she didn't want to remember?

Drawing a deep ragged breath, she slowly lifted her head from the pillow. The bedclothes whispered with her movement as she sat up. Then she froze. Something was moving near the skirting board, where she'd patched the hole. A whimper died in her throat as she stared at the mosaic of swarming shadows.

Her tongue felt rough and powdery, as though she'd swallowed soot. Nausea clenched her stomach and she closed her eyes, blocking out the heaving black mass and with it the fear that the past had found her at last.

The silence pressed into her ears like the roar of a train and she imagined something was shuffling towards her in the dark. If she opened her eyes he might be right in front of her. The Coal-Man. A trickle of sweat scurried down her neck and made her shiver.

She was afraid of what the light might reveal, but even more afraid of what the darkness might hide. Biting her lip, she reached out for the bedside lamp and switched it on, flooding the room with light. She was alone. With an exhausted sigh she sank back into the bed.

For three nights she'd woken to the soft mocking laughter and the sense that she was not alone. She thought of Megan and tasted coal dust, thick and peaty in her throat. Tears welled in her eyes and she pushed the memory away. She rolled onto her side and drew her legs up until she was curled tightly into a ball. As tears began to roll down her cheeks, she tried to banish the certainty that something inside her pillow was drinking them.

In the morning she felt as though someone had replaced her eyelids with sandpaper. She'd managed to fall asleep again for a couple of hours after lying awake most of the night, but it hadn't refreshed her at all. If anything it had only deepened her exhaustion.

She shambled into work half an hour late, having dozed through the alarm and been forced to skip her shower. She felt grimy and unwashed, her limp brown hair hanging in oily strands around her face. The office manager frowned at her arrival and looked with exaggerated puzzlement at her watch, a cynical reproach. As if the law firm would grind to a halt if the file clerk wasn't there at the stroke of eight to help everyone with their ABCs.

The office was hellishly bright, its harsh buzzing fluorescents making Jen's bloodshot eyes throb. She felt like some pale cave-dwelling creature, forced into the overbright world to suffer in its blinding illumination. From the age of twelve the shadows had teemed with menace but over time she had convinced herself that the darkness could be sanctuary. In the light you had to confront things; in the dark, you could hide.

But lately the shadows had begun to whisper again. The feathers in her pillow moved restlessly beneath her head. Things inside the walls chattered busily. And she felt watched even in her sleep. The past haunted her, threatening to destroy the fragile defences she'd spent ten years building.

Dare you to touch the door!

Dare you!

I said it first!

She jerked herself awake as her head lolled painfully onto her shoulder. She'd already caught herself dozing on her feet more than once. Rubbing her eyes, she gathered an armful of files and pushed herself to her feet. Weariness soon overcame her again as she tried to focus on alphabetising them.

It was a shit job like so many other shit jobs she'd got through the agency. But since she hadn't gone to uni, temping was the best she'd managed to come up with for herself. She preferred the kind of work where she didn't come into contact with other people very much and she found the repetitive nature of filing soothing in its mundanity. Companies tended to let their archives get so disorganised no one in the office would be prepared to take on the job of sorting out the chaos. The easiest solution was to hire a temp for a couple of weeks to do the grunt work. This particular job had started three months ago as a two-week assignment, but given the forests of paperwork generated by lawyers, it soon became clear that the firm needed someone full-time.

Jen could hear André, the senior partner, on the phone in the inner office chatting to his wife in French. The lyrical patter of the language was hypnotic and Jen drifted off again. A sheaf of court documents slipped from her fingers, cascading to the floor in an avalanche of fluttering paper. With a muttered curse she knelt and began scooping up the pages. Two gossiping secretaries saw her but made no move to help. She was still on her knees when the door opened. She quickly swept the mess aside and babbled an apology.

"I'm really sorry, André. Let me just get this out of your way."

"It's okay, Jenny," he said.

He pronounced it *Zhen*-nee. At first she'd found it charming; now it just grated. As did his presumptuous use of the childish diminutive. Only her parents had ever called her that and she didn't appreciate the reminder.

André helped her to her feet and kept hold of her arms as though she needed the support. "Is anything wrong? You don't look well."

Stiffening at the unwelcome contact, Jen nevertheless forced a smile. "Just a bad night."

André looked even more worried. "Is Mark bothering you again?" he asked gently. Like a social worker enquiring after a drug problem.

Jen shook her head quickly. Being stalked by her ex-boyfriend had been bad enough, but the shame of everyone in the office knowing had been almost unbearable. André had generously drafted a letter for her threatening legal action if Mark didn't leave her alone, but, while she appreciated his kindness, she hated feeling beholden to anyone. Especially her boss. Even more especially when her boss didn't seem know where the line between work and friendship was. Or pretended he didn't know.

"No, no, he's long gone," she hurriedly reassured him. She swept a hand through her hair as an excuse to pull away. "I just didn't sleep well, that's all."

"I can see that. Listen, why don't you take the rest of the day off? Go home and get some rest."

She relaxed once he got past 'why don't you …' She'd been expecting an invitation to dinner or something equally awkward. But while she couldn't really afford to miss a day's pay, right now sleep was a more pressing need. It wasn't as if she performed any truly vital function in the office anyway.

The files could take the day off too. "Okay. Thanks. Hey, listen, I'm really sorry—"

André waved away the apology. "You have nothing to be sorry about. Just take care of yourself and come back when you feel better."

"I will."

"And if there's ever anything I can do," he said, clasping her hands in both of his. "And I do mean *anything* – you know I'm here for you, right?"

Jen nodded, feeling belittled and embarrassed. As usual, she couldn't tell whether he was making advances or not. Was he being inappropriate? Or just foreign? Or was she just paranoid?

"You can even call me at home if you need to. You have my number."

She did. He'd scribbled it on a business card for her on her second day at work. "I'll be fine," she said, hoping she would be.

The house greeted her with chilly silence when she returned, as though resentful that she had left. Too tired to go upstairs to bed, she collapsed on the sofa. Sleep descended on her within minutes, ferrying her back into the unwelcome past.

*

She heard the scuttling like rats in the walls. Then the bouncing tumble as something found a path through the maze of boards behind the wall adjoining Megan's room. At last it rolled out through the hole in the skirting board and clattered to a stop at the foot of the bed.

A lump of coal.

Jen's skin went slick and clammy as she watched, waiting. Waiting for it to come alive, to unfold long spidery legs and creep towards her, fixing her with tiny glaring eyes on stalks. Or would it swell like a balloon, distorting itself into something vaguely human, something with a grotesque head and black, empty eyes? What form would he take when he finally revealed himself?

The little girl slipped out from under the safety of the duvet, placing her bare feet one at a time on the chilly floorboards. They creaked beneath even her slight weight. Slowly, she inched towards the small fist-sized thing.

A lifeless eye, it stared at her emptily. She swallowed to stop her stomach heaving. She reached for it, so tense she was vibrating. If it flew at her, she'd scream.

Her tiny fingers closed around its cold hardness and she shuddered with revulsion as she hurried across the room with it. No, she hadn't felt it twitch. Definitely not.

Outside, the tree branch tapped like an impatient finger at the window. She raised the sash and threw the coal out into the night where it joined the others gleaming on the wet grass. Like black teeth grinning over a gruesome secret. They were always gone by the morning, leaving her to wonder whether they'd even been there at all.

Slamming the window shut, she dived back under the duvet, scrubbing the black dust off her hand and onto her pyjamas. The smell was stuck in her nose – sharp and oily, like black chalk. She smelled it all the time now. They said it was because of what had happened to Megan, that it was something called a 'hallucination'. What they meant was that it was just in her head.

The coal was gone, but she couldn't sleep. More of it was rattling inside the walls. Gently, like a rain of pebbles and plaster dust. Jen lay frozen, trembling, her eyes blurry with tears. Then, from inside her pillow, she heard him laugh softly.

She scrambled out of bed with a cry and raced down the hall. She tore open her parents' door and hurled herself into their bed, shaking them awake.

Her mother was startled until she saw it was only Jen. Her face softened and she patted her daughter's cheek. "It's okay, Jenny," she said in a singsongy voice.

"What is it now?" her father demanded sleepily.

The Coal-Man

"It's nothing, dear; she's just had a bad dream."

"There's somebody in my room," Jen said in a tiny voice. She was suddenly afraid of being overheard and she didn't dare speak his name aloud. "There's a man inside my pillow."

Her father grunted and turned over noisily, bumping the night table with a curse. "There's nobody in your room and you're too old to be running to us. Go back to bed."

Too old? She was only twelve.

To Jen's mother he growled, "Don't encourage her. She just wants attention. As if she hasn't had enough of that already."

"You'll be fine, sweetie," her mother whispered quickly, derailing her father's train of innuendo before it could gain any more speed. "Go back to bed. Everything will be all right in the morning." She yawned hugely and Jen winced at the warm sour breath. Not just wine tonight.

Jen shuddered as her father muttered something about Megan. Something about how her little sister had never been this difficult, had never caused any problems. Jen heard the resentful question in his tone: Why *her*?

"Good night, Jenny." Her mother held her with stiff, awkward arms for a moment before pushing her away.

Jen hesitated on the threshold before closing their door and padding back down the hall. She should have known they wouldn't believe her. And why should they when no one but Jen could see the coal?

She turned the light on and crawled back into bed, curling into a ball for warmth. Her room was always cold. She pulled the duvet tight up under her chin and squeezed her eyes shut. A soft clatter from the wall made her gasp. She could hear lumps of coal knocking against each other as they rolled out, making their way across the floor towards her. She wept silently into the pillow, terrified to open her eyes. They could fall to the floor, but surely they couldn't climb up into the bed. The laughter came again and she felt something hard beneath her cheek. Reaching inside the pillowcase her fingers encountered a lump of coal. She cried out and felt her bladder let go with a

177

warm stab of shame.

She scrambled to her knees and flung the pillow to the floor. The coal tumbled out and rolled to a stop in front of the hole in the skirting board. There came another soft clatter from there. She stared at the wall, willing it to be silent. She was still staring when the sun came up.

*

The rich colours staining the walls were not the shades of sunrise and Jen blinked at her surroundings, disoriented. It took her a while to realise she was in the living room and not her bedroom. She wasn't even sure what day it was. Had she slept through the night and into the next day?

The two years she'd spent at Lakeview had wrecked her body clock just as it had wrecked the remains of her childhood. She wrinkled her nose. Lakeview. As though it were a holiday home in the Lake District instead of a hospital for crazies.

She fished her phone out of her handbag and it immediately restored her sense of time. It was the same day. André had sent her home from work. And while she'd regressed ten years in her sleep, she'd only closed her eyes for a handful of hours. Sunset was painting the sky and another night was coming.

Tears had dried on her face and she rubbed away the salty tracks. She was haunted by the dream. Even so, she knew it wasn't a dream at all. Megan was dead. Her parents were dead. The past, however, was not.

Megan had always been her parents' favourite. She was the pretty one, blond and blue-eyed, like a little porcelain doll, while Jen was mousy and unremarkable. And with their favourite gone, Jen was only a painful reminder of the place their golden child had occupied in their hearts. They made it obvious to Jen that she could never fill that place, however desperately she tried to get their attention with her sick fairy tales. A man made of coal. A voice in her pillow. It was better for everyone if she just 'went away' for a while.

And she had been fine at Lakeview. Happy, even. The days slipped by like waves, one indistinguishable from the next. Her life was governed by bland routine that she found surprisingly comforting. It was predictable, dependable. Safe. The doctors could find nothing wrong with her, but her parents continued to pay the bills. A year passed and Jen barely noticed.

They had almost managed to convince her that she'd been delusional after all, that there was no Coal-Man, that he was merely a product of her guilt over Megan's death. She needed someone to blame, they said. Then her parents veered onto the wrong side of the carriageway and drove head-on into a lorry. Both were drunk. Both died instantly. Their grief had killed them, people said, clucking in sympathy over poor orphaned Jenny.

When the young pretty policewoman came to see her at Lakeview Jen had reacted with eerie calm to the tragic news. Her only question: "Was there any coal with them?"

The policewoman looked startled. "How did you …?" She furrowed her brow, exchanging an uncomfortable look with the nurse who patted Jen's shoulder reassuringly. A patronising gesture that said *Now, now, I thought we were finished with all that silly talk.*

But the policewoman continued. "As a matter of fact, yes. There were several lumps of coal found at the scene. Do you—"

The nurse drew herself up importantly, her mouth set in a firm line. A look of understanding dawned on the policewoman's face and the question died on her lips. By now Jen was attuned to the secret and silent language of grown-ups and she knew what the look between the women meant. Coal was a key symbol in the family drama. Like a character in a play who stood for Guilt with a capital G. If there was coal at the scene of the accident, there was a rational – a *sane* – explanation for it. There was nothing mystical about it, no need to act surprised. Jen was in here because she was crazy, after all. One mustn't pander to her morbid obsessions.

179

"They must have had it with them because of what happened … last year." The policewoman said, inventing a reason. She squeezed Jen's hand, looking at her with intolerable pity. "I'm very sorry. They didn't suffer."

But Jen knew better. "Oh yes they did," she said, her chest feeling icy and hollow. "The Coal-Man came back for them. And he'll come for me next."

She might just as easily have asked them to keep her locked up for another year.

Eventually they were forced to discharge her. They'd done all they could but it was time for her to rejoin society. They counselled her on grief and guilt and released her into the wild to fend for herself. But no kid could hope to return from such a place untainted. The stigma provided endless ammunition for cruel peers and ignorant teachers alike.

Jen's Aunt Sally came to stay with her in the house until she came of age. Jen was fourteen and, although she liked Sally, her adolescent angst proved more than the poor woman could handle. Jen raged bitterly at the teasing she suffered at school, unfairly taking out her frustrations on her aunt. She delighted in reducing Sally to tears. She couldn't make friends and so she made enemies; it felt good to see someone else in pain for a change. But the shallow victories ultimately made Jen feel even worse and the day after her eighteenth birthday, Sally moved out.

Her parents had preserved Megan's room just as it had been when she died, like a shrine, while Jen's room had been relegated to the junk room. Deeply hurt and angry, Jen stuck a sale sign outside the day Sally left and took whatever she was offered for the contents of the two bedrooms – Megan's and her parents'. Everything else went out with the rubbish.

That was only a few years ago. She'd kept the rooms empty ever since. And she'd been fine. Mostly. Until the coal had begun to rattle in the walls again.

Although she dreaded it, she knew she had to go upstairs and check her bedroom. She stared at the tangle of sheets on the bed and thought of all the nights she'd lain awake there after Megan's death, tormented by voices and the rattle of coal. At Lakeview they'd made her want to believe it was all in her mind. They taught her the magic word 'schizophrenia', which seemed like salvation. It rescued her from the horror by neatly explaining everything away. Jen was an imaginative girl and the trauma of her sister's death had momentarily blurred the line between fantasy and reality for her. Just like that. After all, she'd never actually heard the voice of the Coal-Man until Megan died. And she'd never *seen* him at all.

Jen smoothed the sheets over and lay down on the bed, staring up at the ceiling. The light was dying and she thought of the coal shed. Her parents had demolished it after the tragedy. She closed her eyes and squeezed out a tear.

*

"Hey Megan, know what I heard last night?"

"What?"

"The Coal-Man. He was calling your name."

Megan looked frightened for a moment, but she quickly replaced her fear with bravado. "He was not," she said, not sounding at all certain.

But Jen nodded gravely. "He was. He knocked on my wall and said he was coming for you."

"Stop it or I'm telling," Megan whimpered.

"What's there to tell, snitch? It's the truth. He left me something too. He said to give it to you." Jen held up a lump of coal.

Megan burst into tears. "Stop it, you're scaring me! You made that up!"

"Very well," Jen sighed, pocketing the coal and making as if to leave. "I'll just have to give it back to him and tell him you said he wasn't real."

"Nooo!" Megan wailed. Honestly, she was such a baby, even for a seven-year-old. Jen had just turned twelve and felt

181

positively grown-up.

"Then you have to go tell him you're sorry."

Megan sniffled and wiped her nose on the back of her sleeve. "Will you come with me?"

"Of course, silly."

It was the sisters' favourite game. They waged a campaign of mental torture against each other about the man who lived in the coal shed. Both girls were terrified of the basement shed, of the cascade of coal down the chute as their parents dumped it in from the street once a week, just like in Victorian times. More than anything they dreaded being sent to fetch coal for the fire. The basement was intimidating enough by itself but it was the coal shed they really feared.

"Shed" was an exaggeration. Occupying an area about the size of a doghouse, it was really more of a cupboard. Its rustic door was fitted with an ancient wrought iron latch that required a bit of force to release it from its rusty keep. Opening the door to the shed sometimes loosed a small black avalanche and the girls had convinced themselves that a little man lived inside who wanted to bury them in coal to keep them forever.

The Coal-Man knocked on their walls and whispered to them in the night, always claiming he wanted the other sister. When they were feeling especially brave, they would venture down into the basement and stand before the door, daring one another to knock and see if he was home. They took a perverse delight in scaring each other.

"Go on, Megan, you have to knock."

Megan looked at the small door to the coal shed, unable to hide her fear. Tears shimmered in her eyes as she turned from the door to her sister and back. Jen was always better at pretending bravery in the face of such adventures and she soon grew bored with her sister's reluctance.

"Coward."

"Am not!"

"Then do it. Maybe he's not even home today."

The possibility gave Megan the shred of courage she

needed. She reached out a trembling hand and hesitated for several seconds before finally touching one finger to the wood of the door and instantly yanking it back as though burnt.

Megan beamed triumphantly. "Ha ha, your turn, scaredy-pants!"

"That was never a knock."

But Megan's tiny triumph had empowered her and she regarded her sister with unexpectedly adult seriousness. "He doesn't really need for us to knock," she said. "He knows we're here."

Jen stared at the door, trying hard to hide her nervousness. She knew there wasn't really a Coal-Man, not *really*. She was too old to believe that. It was just something she'd made up to terrorise her sister. Megan had added her own embellishments and the story had taken on a life of its own. But that was all it was – a *story*. Something *not real*.

But sometimes the coal would shift inside by itself. And sometimes Jen was sure it sounded like whispering. Or laughter. And sometimes she was convinced she heard a sinister voice coming from inside her pillow at night.

Her heart hammered in her chest, so fast it hurt. She swallowed and then reached out and rapped the door quickly, before she lost her nerve. A surge of exhilaration raced through her. She couldn't have felt braver if she'd put her hand in a lion's mouth and drawn it back unscathed.

"Now you have to open the door," she told Megan, raising the stakes. She held out the lump of coal. "He wants this back."

Megan's eyes gleamed with both fear and excitement. The game had no rules at all and the only object was fear. Their own as much as each other's.

Megan clenched and unclenched her fist as she edged forwards, priming herself to lift the latch and pull the door open. At last she positioned her fingers beneath the latch and glanced back at her sister for encouragement. Jen watched, spellbound, hardly daring to blink. Megan sucked in a deep breath and held it. Then she pushed the latch up. It sprang free of the catch with a loud click that made both girls jump. Maintaining her determination, Megan pulled the door slowly open.

There was no one inside.

The girls sagged with a mixture of relief and disappointment. Megan gave a little bark of laughter, as though unimpressed by the secret behind a magic trick.

"He's gone," she said matter-of-factly, tossing the lump of coal inside with an irreverence that made Jen uneasy. The shed was nearly empty and the coal clattered with a hollow sound against the brick wall and rolled to rest somewhere in the shadows.

A vague emptiness descended on them. Neither girl really *wanted* there to be a Coal-Man but the anticlimax of his non-existence always left them feeling unfulfilled. Sometimes they were rewarded by the scurrying of a mouse inside as they flung wide the door. And when the shed was full, coal would often spill out, making them shriek with terror and run back up the stairs. They'd collapse on Jen's bed, shaking with helpless laughter before daring each other to go and close the door.

But lately the game had been getting stale for Jen. Megan was always prepared to trust whatever her sister told her and her blind faith was frankly a little tiresome. At the same time, it was unnerving. It was as though she knew things Jen didn't. Some of the things the Coal-Man had allegedly done seemed beyond what Megan could have dreamt up on her own. Like the morning Jen had woken to discover a lump of coal inside her pillow. How had it got there? Jen was a light sleeper, awakened by the slightest noise; she couldn't imagine that her little sister could have sneaked into her room and planted it there while she slept.

And however afraid Megan was at the start of any adventure, by the end it was always Jen who was the more rattled. That had to change. It was time to take things to a new level. Jen had an idea that would require all her courage. It took her nearly a week before she finally had the guts to put it into action.

The night before the Big Scare, Jen knocked softly on the wall between their bedrooms, calling her own name in a low voice. "Jennniferrr … I'm coming for you …"

She pressed her ear against the wall but couldn't hear anything from the other side. She pictured Megan sitting bolt upright in bed, her hands over her mouth to stifle a scream. She had hoped for a startled little gasp – something to verify that Megan had heard the Coal-Man call Jen's name this time instead of hers. But there was only silence.

Jen kept it up for a little while before tiring of it. Then, using the lump of coal she'd taken from the fireplace that night, she scrawled a note to Megan on a piece of newspaper. *I have your sister*, it said in jagged charcoal letters. She debated whether to add anything else but decided that would be enough to send Megan tiptoeing to the door of the coal shed, where Jen, dressed all in black, would be waiting to leap out at her. Giggling at her wicked plan, Jen finally went to bed, setting her alarm to wake her before the rest of the house stirred. It would be the Best Scare Ever.

Just before five, she slipped her note under Megan's door and crept downstairs. It was a Saturday, which meant their parents would be sleeping off their hangovers till well past noon. But Megan would be up with the dawn chorus and in the kitchen picking all the raisins out of the cereal as she settled down to breakfast in front of the cartoons. Well, at least that would be her plan. Until she saw the note.

Jen unbolted the basement door and peered down into the chilly depths. It was just a basement, she reassured herself. Just a room in the house like all the others. And in it was a little shed for coal. There was nothing scary about it. Most important of all, there was no Coal-Man. She knew because she'd made him up. With that she marched down the stairs and went straight to the door of the shed without stopping.

She hesitated only a moment before throwing it open. The

shed was full again and her action dislodged a few lumps of coal that had rolled down the pile and come to rest against the inside of the door. The movement startled her but she scoffed at herself.

"It's just coal," she whispered.

She kicked the stray lumps away from the door and out into the middle of the room where Megan would see them. Then she crept inside the shed and shoved her way into the coal to make room for herself. There was no handle on the inside but she managed to pull the door into its frame by grasping the horizontal crossbeams with her fingertips. She heard the latch clack down onto the top edge of the keep. It wouldn't lock without being forced down, but it was still creepy to be inside.

The confinement was oppressive and she felt instantly grimy as the dust and smell from a hundred years' worth of coal settled around her. It was a sharp, unpleasant odour, chalky and metallic like the old steam trains their father loved. She wished she could see her sister's face as she discovered the note from the Coal-Man and timidly made her way down the stairs to the shed.

A week later Jen wished she'd never had the idea at all.

As with any game of one-upmanship, Megan knew she had to top Jen's performance and the only way to do that was to build on it. Only Jen didn't want her performance topped. Megan had screamed when Jen leapt out of the shed, howling demonically and raining fistfuls of coal at her. Her screams had dissolved into huge gulping sobs that eventually gave way to manic laughter as she realised it was only her sister.

Jen could almost see the gears turning in her sister's head over the next few days, see the scheming behind mischievous eyes. So when Megan clumsily shoved a note under Jen's door the following weekend (*I HAVE MEGAN!* screamed the charcoal capitals), Jen simply rolled her eyes and ignored the bait. *Copycat*, she thought. The game was old anyway and she wanted to go to the park to play with Susie and Fiona, who were her own age. She couldn't hang around with her kid sister all the time.

On her way downstairs she paused at the basement door and thought of Megan shivering down there in the chilly shed, her nerves on edge as she waited for Jen to come looking for her. How long would she wait before getting either too scared or too bored? Probably all of five minutes, Jen thought, perversely pleased with herself for having stayed in the scary shed herself for nearly half an hour. It had been full of coal when she'd done it and the shed was empty now.

She got home just after dark. Mum was already halfway through a bottle of wine and Dad was slumped sullenly in front of a match on TV, muttering rude things at the players who couldn't hear him. Megan was nowhere to be seen. She couldn't still be hiding. But she was probably angry with Jen for spoiling her scare, so perhaps she was hiding somewhere else. Jen searched the house to no avail. She didn't become alarmed until her mother said she hadn't seen Megan all day, had assumed she was at the park with Jen.

Jen's blood turned to ice-water and she made her feet carry her to the basement. Down the stairs. To the door of the coal shed. Where she breathed a sigh of relief. It was latched. There was no way to lock the door from inside. But she still felt a sense of disquiet. Something tugged at the back of her mind, a detail she couldn't quite recall. Coal dust hung in the air, so the shed must have been refilled recently.

Without really knowing why, she prised the latch up and opened the door. A scream froze in her throat as coal spilled out of the shed and onto the floor around her feet, scuttling over her sister's lifeless body like rats.

*

Jen surfaced from the memory and wiped away her tears. If only she hadn't been so stubborn. If only she'd let Megan get her own back. If only, if only, if only. Those 'if onlys' had lodged like splinters in her heart and she'd spent ten years trying to pull them out.

The rattling in the wall wouldn't let her forget. She stared at the discolouration in the skirting board. She'd patched the hole there with papier-mâché. A useful skill she'd learnt at Lakeview. And how therapeutic it had been to seal that up. But now she thought she could see movement there, as of something stirring beneath a sheet, straining to emerge. A voice whispered her name.

Jen squeezed her eyes shut. *There's nothing there*, she told herself. *Just my mind playing tricks like before.* She didn't want to be crazy but it was preferable to the alternative.

Something thumped heavily against her inexpert repair. Like a rock thrown against the side of a tent. Then another. And another. Her eyes flew open. The newspaper was bulging out away from the skirting board and she watched in horror as a tiny fissure opened. Behind it she could see only black. At last the pressure split the paper enough for the coal to force its way out. Several lumps came tumbling out like black gumballs from a filthy machine. They clattered to a stop and lay on the floor like a rank of chess pieces.

Tears stung her eyes as she realised how alone and isolated she was. There was no one she could turn to, no one she could call. The police wouldn't respond to a summons about coal in her bedroom. She might as well call the doctors at Lakeview to bundle her into a quiet room for the rest of her days. And if she *was* imagining all this, surely that's where she belonged.

Inside the wall the coal shifted, restless.

Jen crept off the bed and edged towards the coal. It lay between her and the door like a challenge. She took a deep breath and stepped gingerly over it. When nothing happened she hurried across the floor and out of the room, slamming the door shut behind her.

She ran down the stairs and into the kitchen. With trembling hands she dug through the piles of bills and other paperwork until she found what she was looking for. Then she picked up the phone.

"André? It's me. Um – Jen."

There followed a weighty pause. She imagined him looking around fearfully, covering the phone with one hand and seeing if the ringing had woken his wife.

"Jenny?" he whispered, sounding bewildered.

"I'm really sorry to ring you so late, but I didn't know who else to call. And well, you said if I ever needed anything …"

Another pause. Had she called some bluff? Had he not really meant it?

"Yes, yes, of course," he recovered quickly. "Of course it's okay. I was just …" He yawned. "What time is it?"

"Just past midnight. Listen, I hate to ask this of anyone, but I really need your help. I need someone to tell me I'm not crazy. Or that I *am*. Either way it's not something I can do by myself."

"Of course, of course." He was waking up. "What do you need me to do?"

She swallowed. "Can you come over?" She loathed asking, loathed *needing* to ask.

"It can't wait until morning?"

"No, it can't. I need …" Her voice broke and she forced the words out. "I need someone here now. Please?"

As much as she hated the wheedling tone in her voice she also hoped it quashed any chance that he'd mistake her call for an invitation for sex. She gave him her address and rang off.

He was there in ten minutes, looking rumpled, unshaven and sleepy. He hadn't dressed for a midnight assignation and Jen felt a pang of guilt for thinking the worst of him. If she'd been wrong about him, what else might she have been wrong about?

"I know this will sound crazy, but all I need you to do is go upstairs and open a door and tell me what you see. I'll explain afterwards."

His eyebrows climbed to his hairline and he peered up the stairs, curious and apprehensive. "Shouldn't you call the police? If it's an intruder—"

She shook her head fiercely. "It's nothing like that. It may

189

be nothing at all. Please, André."

"Very well," he said at last. "Which door?"

"The first one. Just tell me if there's anything on the floor by the wall on the right."

He climbed the stairs, glancing down at Jen from time to time. She clung to the banister, eyes wide as she watched. Then she held her breath as he reached her bedroom door. He pushed it open and stepped inside, disappearing from sight behind the door.

Seconds passed like years and she finally called up to him. "Is there anything there?"

"Looks like you've got mice," he said amiably. "Or rats. They've made a hole in your wall."

"Is there anything by the hole?"

"Yes. Some stones. Or – no. That's strange. I think it's coal."

Jen's stomach twisted. Real. All of it was real. *He* was real. From her position at the base of the stairs she heard the angry rattling inside the wall above her. There was a splintering of boards and then what sounded like a violent hailstorm as coal surged into the bedroom.

"André, get out of there!" she cried.

But he was already screaming.

Jen forced herself up the stairs but she knew it was too late. She shouldered her way into the room and stared in horror at what she saw. The wall had been torn apart by the force and a thunderous deluge of coal was pouring through. A black mountain was forming where the small hole had once been and coal flowed around it, spreading to cover the floor. All she could see of André was a hand, weakly grasping at the air as he drowned in the black flood. There was nothing she could do.

The coal was already accumulating around her ankles and she slid her feet through it as if through heavy snow. The door had been forced shut again by the weight of the coal. The cold metallic smell was overpowering. A peaty taste filled Jen's mouth and she coughed dryly, bringing up gobs of black spit.

The level soon reached her hips. Her legs were completely immobilised and she flailed helplessly as she tried to dig herself out.

Through the fog of dust she could see movement beyond the ruined wall. The coal wasn't coming from inside the wall itself but from Megan's room. Jen hadn't gone in there since she'd emptied and sealed it years ago. But something was in there now.

The fall of coal had lessened and soon it stopped completely. She heard a clatter as something moved in the rubble, dislodging lumps of coal. A thin figure emerged from the haze, its jerky movements like those of a crippled animal crawling away from a trap. The shape was vaguely human, but hideously disfigured. Its arms and legs flopped uselessly as though attached by threads. It moved by wriggling its torso, half crawling, half sliding, gradually making its way across the landscape of coal to where Jen was trapped. The movement appeared to cause it immense pain. A rasping cry came from its shattered mouth with every exertion.

The creature finally came to rest on one side and turned its baleful gaze on Jen. Filthy ropes of hair hung about its mutilated face and Jen covered her mouth, biting back a scream as she recognised it. It was Megan.

Dust floated in the air and the smell took Jen back to that awful night in the basement. She remembered Megan's broken limbs, her crushed skull, her staring eyes dusted black with soot. She imagined her sister's terror as coal rained down on her from the chute above, pinning her under its weight, burying her alive. How long had it taken? How long had she lain there hoping someone would come? And how much must she have cursed her sister for spurning her?

Tears carved pale lines through the soot on Jen's face. "Please," she whimpered.

But the piercing black eyes conveyed only hatred. The shattered mouth worked, forming hellish sounds but no words.

Jen knew what it was saying, however. At last she

understood. There was no Coal-Man. There never had been. The missing memory slotted into place as she stared at her sister's bent and blackened fingers.

"Yes," she whispered. "I pushed the latch down that morning."

It felt good to remember it, but it felt better to say it, to relieve the pressure that one simple act had created within her all those years. She hadn't known their parents would refill the shed that day, but that hardly mattered. She'd locked Megan in the place that would become her tomb. It was such a simple act, latching a door. So easily forgotten.

The mangled figure twitched forward, reaching for Jen with one slack arm. Jen recoiled with a scream and the broken fingers were instantly thrust inside her open mouth. The sound they made as she bit down was like that of an iron latch sliding home into its keep.

MEA CULPA

Kate Farrell

Consider please, the theory of chaos: a butterfly flaps its wings in Japan, and here in London your lover tries to kill you.

Alex and I had been living together for four years. We were a handsome couple, both tall and fair, with strong profiles. Our high brows and patrician noses might have belonged on a coin and, like monarchs, we believed in never complain, never explain. We were occasionally taken for brother and sister, and as the idea of incest amused us, we would sometimes gently torture strangers with the notion that perhaps our relationship was not what it appeared. Our work was tolerable, our mortgage bearable, our friends genial, our families scattered. Child bearing and rearing was not yet an option, although we would consider the possibility and toy with names. I recall Clovis and Rapunzel were favourites for a while. It was more of a parlour game than a serious declaration of intent. Everything was perfection. Perfection: define it. A state of grace? Perhaps, yet that seems too Catholic. Is perfection the absence of badness or the presence of goodness? Goodness: again, define it. It would be possible, but not in the least desirable, to play these futile word games forever, or to become the armchair philosopher. The truth is that I find myself in a very strange place. I cannot recall how I arrived, and the ticket seems to have no return portion. That was careless of me.

For Alex and I, our home, our redoubt, was a split-level apartment in a converted warehouse, sublimely ill equipped to deal with children. As were we. There was a terrace, which overlooked a canal to the west of London, and in the cooler weather the smell from the water was barely perceptible. We loved the large windows, the oak floors, the soundproofed space where we could laugh, scream, twist and shout to our hearts' content, as the need arose. Most of all, we loved ourselves. Or so I thought.

Some months ago, Alex was holding the lift door open. It was an elderly if effective device with an interior concertina door, and as I entered, the door closed on my fingers. The pain, for a split second was like having teeth drilled without anaesthetic, my nerve endings were laid bare, and I thought I might faint. Alex looked at me, or through me, I couldn't decide which, as the pain had scrambled my vision. The next thing I recall was holding my hand under an ice-cold running tap, with a suitably concerned Alex, ministering to my needs.

I heard, "Sorry, the door just slipped …" I was in no mood to care.

At work the next day, fingers swollen and taped up, I was reminded by the doom merchants that those old-fashioned lifts, though perfect in a Hitchcock film and wonderfully atmospheric, can be a death trap. I let some of the girls fuss over me, but didn't reveal how the door had actually slipped. I wonder why.

Alex cooked a superb meal by way of an apology, and it seemed better not to discuss the incident; incidents do happen, as surely as accidents. Who was it that said there are no accidents? Somebody. Besides neither of us cared much for soul-searching, (never complain, never explain) or angst ridden post-mortems. And the food was to die for.

Several weeks later, as spring stuttered into summer, my fingers had healed and the incident was all but forgotten. I mentioned that a work colleague had invited me to play in a mixed doubles event at their tennis club. Alex hated tennis with a passion, so I had accepted the invitation without conferring. We would occasionally go our separate ways socially, as not all our interests were mutual. In fact that seemed to be one of the great strengths of our relationship.

194

"Sam Ryan's asked me to play in a mixed doubles thing on Saturday."

Alex followed a piece of Roquefort round the plate, pushed the plate away, eyed me.

"Ah, the lovely Sam. Am I invited too?"

"Christ no, you'd hate it, you hate tennis."

"I see." A sip from the wineglass. "So, you and Sam, and who else …?"

"Don't know. We've not played with each other before …"

"As it were," said my lover. I hated these cheap shots, so it was my turn to eye Alex; petty I know, but there is always room for small-mindedness, even in the grandest passion.

"Out with it," I said.

Alex stabbed at the cheese. What had it done to provoke such a mauling?

"I thought we were going to start work on the back bedroom?"

I held my ground, unaware of the shifting sands.

"We've been threatening to do that since Christmas, one more weekend won't make much difference. Anyway, I think I quite fancy the exercise."

The poor cheese was subjected to a further attack.

"Alright, you go and have your fun with Sam; you spend all week at work together, beats me why you'd want to spend the weekend too, but it's your choice." Cut, slash, stab. "I'll start the room on my own."

I loved Alex dearly, however interior decoration was not, what you might call, a strength. Plenty of enthusiasm, little finesse. I had designed our home with some care and flair with Alex as an occasional labourer, fetcher of brew and biscuits, and manipulator of stiff shoulders. Foolish, but I snorted with derision.

"Er, I don't think so …"

At that point, Alex plunged the cheese knife into the back of my hand.

Hindsight is not a benefit – it is a curse. Should I have been kinder, more appreciative, less impatient? Should I have been taller, shorter, older, younger, fatter, thinner? Can I recall a time I was aware of that subtle shift, which would later herald the tsunami? Was I that self-absorbed that Alex's needs were a poor second to mine? Was it all my fault? Yes, it must have been. I hadn't willingly or knowingly transgressed, I thought I had been charming, helpful, supportive, loving. I *thought* I had. With the benefit of this thing called hindsight would I have acted differently at any time? I don't think so.

There was no tennis that weekend.

That same Christmas, when we had discussed the redecoration of the spare bedroom, I had been the reluctant recipient of a Caithness paperweight, whose design resembled a lilac coloured foetus preserved in aspic. As it was a gift from Alex's purblind mother, it remained on display on a floating shelf, despite my periodic endeavours to consign it to a less prominent position. One Sunday, I was sitting reading the papers, or rather trying to. Alex had been overlooked for a promotion at work the previous week and as an unwitting by-product, eggshells had replaced the reclaimed floorboards in our apartment. I was aware of constant movement as I took cover behind the Sunday Times: pacing, swearing, endless cups of coffee.

Suddenly Alex said, "Catch!" and threw this paperweight at me. I was in mid fold of the property section, both hands were in play, and didn't manage to catch the projectile; instead I arrested its progress with my left ear. There was some swelling and considerable bruising, both of which ultimately healed. The headaches stopped eventually but a strange ringing continued in the ear, which my doctor thought may well be permanent.

After all these episodes there was remorse, a perfect meal or a carefully chosen gift by way of apology, and a promise of no repetition of the event. There were never tears, although there was gentleness. Doctors inspected injuries, we fabricated stories, and returned home to our halogen-lit battlefield. I loved Alex horribly. I wished to create no possibility of friction, I did the best I could to keep our relationship on an even keel, but each time I quizzed myself: what have I done to provoke these attacks? I remembered birthdays, and anniversaries; I enquired after Alex's harridan of a mother; I was punctual; I praised when necessary; I showed proper concern; I shared. It must have been something so subtle, some transgression that was imperceptible to any, other than Alex's keen eye. The fault must have been mine, and yet I was so afraid of further destabilising the fragility of the relationship that I did not dare ask. Life with these minor incidents was preferable to life without Alex.

Though the accidents were some months apart, friends and work colleagues were beginning to ask awkward questions, which I navigated as best I could. Strangely, I felt no need to unburden myself to anyone, and I found the only consolation I required was from Alex. As the summer sun poured into our home like molten butter and I closed the blinds on the giant windows, it was as if I was closing my eyes to the situation, and we settled to our life of disharmony without the disapproval or pity of outsiders. Last month, for instance, Alex and I were attempting to pass each other on the staircase when I carelessly lost my footing and slipped backwards down the last few stairs; it seemed simpler to take a few days off work, rather than explain my arm in a sling, and I was even able to make light of it, while being driven to hospital for what transpired was only a slight dislocation. And it served me right for wearing those ludicrous flip-flops.

"The nurses will be asking if I shouldn't get a season ticket," I said. Alex was not amused and no meal or gift, by way of apology was forthcoming. In fact, I apologised to Alex; it seemed a wiser course.

Mea Culpa

It could have continued; I refused to whine or indulge in bouts of self-pity, and I was ready to acknowledge that the fault was mine, and Alex's actions were as a result of my provocation. It could have continued, if I had not made the mistake of standing in the way when Alex was reversing the Audi. I was next to a pillar in the underground car park, thinking about theatre tickets I had reserved, *Othello* at the Globe, a perfect way to spend a summer's evening. It was a small apology for the incident on the stairs. Yes, I was aware of the car backing towards me, while Alex attempted a precarious manoeuvre in the confined space, and of course I did not assist matters by being so blatantly in the way, but nothing, nothing at all could have prepared me for the sensation as the bumper crushed my legs against the pillar, and then the boot pushed and crashed against my chest as I fell forwards. There was a moment of respite in that dimly lit car park, when Alex must have realised the mistake, and drove forward, releasing me. Was there a fault with the gears? The car reversed again, while I was still doubled over from the first impact. No, nothing could have prepared me for that. I was mashed – there is no other word for it – against the pillar again, my legs, my wrists, my forearms turned to liquid, and my ribs were reduced to splinters. My chest no longer seemed able to provide the wherewithal to breathe, which was baffling. One moment I was standing imagining Alex's delight when I produced the theatre tickets, and the next there was nothing but pain. The colour of pain is white.

Now I have plenty of time to contemplate the events that brought me to this place. What did I do wrong? It's a simple enough question, and until now one I was never brave enough to ask.

I lie here, stitched into my favourite Armani suit; it hides the devastation done to my body, which was broken beyond repair. The funeral directors reassembled the pile of sticks and mush that had been my torso; they padded and moulded to make me fit for viewing. Fortunately my face was unmarked, so Alex, my lovely Alexandra was able to bend over and kiss me goodbye. I felt her soft lips brush the light stubble on my cheeks, for it is true, the hair and beard do continue to grow after death. I know that now.

Lightning Source UK Ltd.
Milton Keynes UK
176092UK00001B/5/P